LAWFULLY DASHING

JENNA BRANDT

*Dedicated to
my husband, Dustin, Badge #5654,
who inspired me to create this series.
You're not only my heart and soul,
but my own personal lawkeeper.*

This is a work of fiction. Names, characters, organizations, places, events and incidents are either products of the author's imagination or are used fictitiously. Locale and public names are sometimes used for atmospheric purposes. Any resemblance to actual persons, living or dead, actual events, or actual locations is purely coincidental. All rights reserved.

No part of this book may be reproduced, or stored in a retrieval system, or transmitted in any form or by any means, electronic, mechanical, photocopying, recording, or otherwise, without express written permission of the author, except in the case of brief quotations embodied in critical reviews and certain other noncommercial uses permitted by copyright law. For permission requests, email jenna@jennabrandt.com.

Text copyright © Jenna Brandt 2018.

ONE

Clear Mountain Resort was filled with tourists as Brooke Patterson and her two friends entered the lobby. Not surprising, considering the Colorado vacation spot was a popular destination for Christmas break.

Brooke was still surprised her friends talked her into coming over from Boulder, considering she had been looking forward to a weekend at home, binge-watching Netflix and eating popcorn.

The trio moved over to stand in the ten-deep check-in line, avoiding bumping into people as they passed through the packed lobby.

"Can you believe all these people? I expected it to be busy, but not this much. This place must be booked out to capacity," Kristen Tucker, a dispatcher for the Boulder County police department, stated.

Brooke and Kristen worked together and bonded over the fact they both grew up on the East coast. When Brooke heard Kristen's thick Boston accent over the dispatch radio, she knew she had found an ally on the department, an ally Brooke needed considering she was a female in a predominantly male occupation. Cops were hard on rookies, but even more so, when they were women.

Not wanting to think about her job while on vacation, Brooke changed the subject by saying, "I hope we get to do everything we want. I know we booked our spa day and restaurant reservations ahead of time, but getting ski time in might be a different story."

"Don't be such a pessimist," Trina Vasquez, Brooke and Kristen's friend from the gym, chastised playfully. "We'll figure out a way to make it work. Between the three of us, we represent every man's fantasy. A little flirting will go a long way."

Brooke shook her head. Trina was a natural-born flirt. It was as easy to her as breathing air, but Brooke couldn't figure out how to do it without feeling awkward.

Her friend was right about her statement about their appearances though. With Trina's long brown hair, hazel eyes, and a killer smile, she was an exotic beauty. Kristen was a knock-out with red hair, green eyes and a voluptuous body. Men often commented when they were together she looked like a real-life Jessica Rabbit. Brooke rounded out the three women with her shoulder-length blonde hair, blue eyes, and sporty physique.

"You would think that," Kristen stated with a roll of her eyes. "But I highly disagree. Flirting can't get everything all the time."

"It can if you do it right," Trina corrected. "And believe me, *I* do it right."

Kristen and Brooke both smirked at her, wagging their fingers in a shame-shame gesture and making a teasing "ew" sound.

"I didn't mean it like *that*," Trina said with her face turning red. "I'm a good Christian girl, after all. I just mean being friendly helps."

"It does. But there's friendly, and then there's… *friendly*," Kristen clarified with a wag of her eyebrows. "You definitely fall on the latter end of that spectrum."

"I should be mad, but when you're right, you're right," Trina stated with a laugh, causing the other two friends to join in.

"My, my, what's so funny? I'm dying to know," a deep male voice said from behind them.

The trio turned to face the stranger who was watching them with deep interest. He was handsome with sandy blond hair and a chiseled body. The problem was he knew it. Brooke's radar went off. She got the sleaze vibe the moment she made eye contact with him. He carried himself in a way that made it obvious he wanted women to notice him.

"Aren't one of you going to tell me?" the stranger asked.

Trina was a sucker for a guy in a tight t-shirt and replied without hesitation, "Oh, my friends were harassing me because I'm too friendly."

"No way," he said, shaking his head, "there's no such thing as too friendly."

"That's what I said," Trina said with a flirtatious smile. "See, great minds think alike."

"What are you doing later after you check-in?" he asked with a sleazy grin.

"Oh, we're just—"

Brooke cut Trina off before she gave out too much information to a stranger. "We've got plans," she stated assertively with her cop voice.

Trina pressed her lips together and gripped her hands in front of her. She shrugged. "Brooke's protective of our time; girl's trip and all."

"Oh, I didn't mean to cause a problem. I was here with friends and I figured it would be fun to hang out with you guys; that is, if you're interested."

Brooke shook her head and crossed her arms.

"My friend said it best; girl's trip. We've got the whole weekend full."

He put his hands up in surrender. "Okay, no worries. Have a good weekend."

Brooke turned back around as the line moved forward.

Kristen leaned over and inquired in a whisper, "What was that all about?"

"My cop senses were triggered by that guy," Brooke stated with a frown. "He said he was here with friends, but where were they? I didn't see anyone with him. Besides, he was way too pushy for my liking."

"Ever since Brad, if a guy simply looks your way, they are way too pushy," Kristen countered. "You need to move on and not let that jerk ruin the rest of your life. Stop turning away every opportunity to find someone new."

Trina leaned in towards her friends and whispered, "I agree. I'm not sure what your problem was with the guy behind us. He seemed super nice."

"Ugh, you would think that," Brooke stated with irritation. "You have the worst taste in guys."

"Hey, now, no reason to be mean. I know I'm lousy when it comes to weeding out the bad ones, but that's why I have you, Brooke."

The older female desk clerk smiled at them.

"Good afternoon. Welcome to Clear Mountain Resort. My name is Cindy. How may I help you?"

"We're here to check in," Trina stated with a smile. "The reservation is under Vasquez."

The woman clicked away on the computer in front of her, then looked up. "It seems your suite isn't ready, Ms. Vasquez."

Trina's face scrunched up in confusion before she looked down at her phone in her hand. "It says check-in is at three p.m. It's 3:30," Trina complained.

"One of our maids called in sick today, delaying the cleaning of some rooms. We apologize."

"Our spa reservation isn't until 5:30," Kristen explained. "We were going before our dinner reservation at 8:30. What can we do in the meantime?"

It figures we can't get into our room. I was looking forward to relaxing before all the activities Trina had planned, Brooke fumed internally.

"You could go skiing? Or have a bite in the café?"

"No, my friend said we have dinner reservations," Trina interjected. "We don't want to ruin our appetites for dinner. We heard the chef here is amazing. Besides, there's nowhere to change into our snow gear or even enough time to go skiing, anyway."

The woman contemplated the situation for a moment, then suggested, "We offer a horse-drawn sleigh ride. If you like, I can check and see if anyone has it booked right now?"

Trina turned to her friends and asked, "What do you guys think?"

Both women shrugged as Kristen stated, "What can it hurt? At least it would kill time until we can go to the spa."

"Fine, check to see if there is an opening," Trina said in a frustrated tone. "I didn't imagine going on a sleigh-ride for our first part of the trip."

"Who knows, it could be fun," Kristen said in her normal upbeat way. "I'm always up for a new adventure."

The clerk clicked away on the computer again, and a few seconds later looked up with a huge smile. "You guys are in luck. It seems there was a cancellation this afternoon. One of our guests didn't show up today. As compensation for the inconvenience regarding your suite, we will take care of the cost of the ride."

Trina nodded, and the clerk gave them directions how to get to the back part of the resort where the sleigh depot was located.

TWO

Liam Davis watched as a group of three women approached his wooden sleigh. He let out a heavy sigh, realizing they looked like another bunch of self-centered city girls coming into town to get away from it. Not that he resented the need for a break, he just didn't like the snobby attitude that often accompanied the people who came from the city. He had left that life behind four years ago when he got in his car and drove out of New York and ended up in Colorado.

Two years after learning to work with horses on a ranch, Liam took his savings and started his own sleigh ride company. Four horses, two sleighs, and a year later, he was in business.

"Good afternoon, ladies. My name is Liam and I will be your sleigh driver today. I will take you on a horse-drawn tour of the property and along the mountainside."

Trina giggled as she leaned to her friends and said, "The hotel clerk didn't mention the sleigh driver was a hunk."

"Right, maybe we wouldn't have been so upset if we had known he would look like that," Kristen agreed.

It will be a long ride with these women, Liam thought with irritation. *I didn't plan on being a piece of eye-candy for the rest of the day.*

It wasn't the first time women had fawned all over him. With his tall frame, hazel eyes, thick brown hair, and stubbled beard to match, he often got admiring looks. The problem was that he wasn't interested.

He needed to focus on doing his job. The tips were always better if he was polite with the guests. He reached out and helped first the redhead, then the brown-haired woman, and the blonde last. Liam took her hand and felt a tingling sensation.

Before he could analyze what was happening, the blonde slipped on the ice and stumbled forward. Unable to catch her balance, she tumbled towards the ground. Liam swiftly moved to grab her, keeping her from hitting the ice below.

As she lay cradled in his arms, Liam stared into

her beautiful blue eyes. She looked shocked and slightly uncomfortable, possibly from his proximity, but he couldn't bring himself to let her go. She felt like she belonged in them.

The woman put her hands up and pushed back on his chest, righting herself. She averted her eyes and said, "Thank you for catching me. I'm sure I would have broken something if I hit that ice."

"Good thing that didn't happen," Kristen said with a smirk. "The other cops would never let you live that down."

"No kidding," she said as she put her hand on the edge of the sleigh and pulled herself up inside. "I don't need one more thing for them to make fun of when I'm working a call."

"You're a cop?" Liam inquired with surprise. The blonde woman was getting more intriguing every moment he was around her.

She nodded her head. "Yes, have been for the past five years."

"That's impressive," he stated with admiration. "You don't meet a lot of female cops."

"Yes, it's a tough gig, but I love it." She gave him a tentative smile and added, "I'm Brooke, by the way."

He reached out and shook her hand. "Nice to meet you, Brooke."

She gestured to the other women. "These are my friends, Trina and Kristen."

"Nice to meet both of you," he said, taking each of their hands and shaking them. He then handed them several blankets, which they arranged on their laps.

He hopped up into the front seat of the sleigh and prompted his horse, Tinker, to trot. The sleigh took off down the path, ushering in the jingle of the bells.

"The lodge was built fifty-five years ago by a family from Clear Mountain," Liam explained. "They wanted it to be a destination that brought tourists from all over the world. The building you first entered was originally a single story. The family added the second level in the seventies and the additional two wings on either side a decade ago. The main lodge is comprised of the lobby, the grand ballroom, two conference rooms, two wings of suites, and the fine-dining restaurant."

"That's impressive that one family could do all of that," Kristen said with awe.

"Yes, the Wellingtons are a wonderful family. Everyone here loves them. The staff has been lucky they've been able to keep it in the family all these years. Often big corporations come in and buy them up."

"That's sad," Brooke stated.

"It is, but the locals and tourists both like how the Wellingtons keep this place authentic. We get many people who book it for weddings, especially during the spring and summer."

"Oh, how romantic," Trina said with a sigh. "This would be a beautiful place to get married."

He kept the reins for Tinker in one hand while pointing to another building as they passed it. "That's where the heated indoor pool is located. It was the first of its kind in the region. There are also ten private cabins on the property along with two tennis courts, and the lifts to six ski slopes of various difficulties."

The sleigh continued to move, and soon the buildings became dots behind them. They were gliding along the path on the edge of Clear Mountain. As the sleigh headed into the mountain pass, the trees grew thicker and the snow higher on the sides of the cleared road.

"Where do you keep the horses?" Brooke asked with curiosity. "I didn't see a stable anywhere on the tour."

Not surprising she realized the lack of stables. She was a cop after all. It was their job to notice all the details.

"I have a property right up the road. I keep my horses and sleighs there," he said over his shoulder.

"Ah, that makes sense," Brooke stated. "I don't know why I thought you would stay on the property."

"Wishful dreaming?" Trina teased. "It would make it easier to find him if you were looking."

"Well, I'm not. I was just curious. Call it my natural cop mind."

"It's true. You're always the one to catch all the mistakes in movies," Kristen stated. "You notice everything."

"I'm not sure that's a compliment," Brooke said defensively. "Geez, is it gang up on Brooke day?"

Trying to keep a fight from happening, Liam asked, "Where are you all from?"

"We're from Boulder," Kristen informed him. "We're here for the weekend before it gets crazy with Christmas Eve on Wednesday."

"Well, it's good you made reservations. This is a busy time of year for the resort," Liam explained.

There was a turnout Liam used to loop around and head back towards the resort. The clouds above were gray and getting darker by the moment. The news had said snow was in the forecast so he needed to get Tinker home and in her stall before it got too dangerous to be out. Snow drifts could build to several feet tall within a couple of hours.

They reached the back of the resort and Liam

hopped down from the sleigh. He helped the women out of the back.

"I hope you enjoyed your tour," he said with a grin, hoping it presented as grateful.

"Oh, we did. We *really* enjoyed *all* the sights," Trina said with a flirty smile. "It was well worth the delay of getting checked-in," she added as she handed him some money.

He didn't want to take the tip from the woman but figured it would be more awkward if he tried to hand the money back. Reluctantly, he placed it in the front pocket of his jeans.

"All of you be safe. There's supposed to be a lot of snow tonight. Don't get caught in it."

The women nodded their heads as Liam climbed back into his sleigh and took off. He resisted the urge to turn around and take a final look at the pretty blonde he just left behind him.

THREE

"What did you think of our sleigh driver?" Trina asked with her face down on the massage table. "I think he's exactly what you need to get over Brad."

Brooke wanted to focus on her massage without talking, but if she didn't respond, Trina would just keep pestering her.

"He's nice. But you know I'm not interested in dating right now."

"Trina's right, though. You should totally attempt to bump into him again. He's super-hot in that rugged outdoorsy way," Kristen said on the other side of Brooke.

"You guys really need to stop trying to set me up everywhere we go. I'm fine with being single. I need to focus on my job, particularly if I want to be ready for the next time testing for detective opens up."

"There you go again, always talking about work. You sound like a broken record," Trina stated with audible frustration. "Ever since Brad cheated on you, all you do is focus on your job."

Kristen gasped. "Trina, we all agreed not to talk about what Brad did. You shouldn't have brought it up."

"It doesn't matter," Brooke stated, trying to keep from letting the tears fall from the sting of being reminded of what her ex-boyfriend did. "It's been over a year, and I need to stop being so sensitive about it."

"All right, ladies, we're all done here," Brooke's masseuse stated as she ended her final run of pats on Brooke's back. "We will head out and let you get in your robes, then the estheticians will be in to finish with your facials."

An hour later, the women finished with their spa time, and headed back to their suite to get ready for dinner. The wind was whistling outside, and the snow whipped around in spirals as Brooke looked out the window.

What started out as just a standard snowfall had turned into a full-fledged storm. Brooke didn't get nervous often, but the thought of getting stranded made her heart race with apprehension. People got dangerous when they panicked, and she didn't like being trapped with a bunch of unpredictable strangers.

She dabbed on the last of her minimal makeup, and took a last look at her black slacks and red sweater before making her way into the common sitting area of the suite.

No one else was there yet. Not surprising considering her friends took a significantly longer time to get ready than she did. She went over to the counter by the table and poured herself a glass of water, then walked over to the couch and took a seat.

Without her wanting it to, her mind drifted back to the ruggedly good-looking sleigh driver from earlier in the day. She didn't like to admit it, even to herself, but there was something about him that peaked her interest. Perhaps it was the fact he seemed self-assured but not cocky, like he knew who he was but didn't need to flaunt it. Or it could be the fact he didn't seem to mind she was a cop.

Most men were intimidated by her badge and uniform, including her ex-boyfriend. He never admitted it, but she suspected it was the reason he went looking for a woman to stroke his ego. She never meant to make him feel inferior, but he had stated as much.

She could still remember every word from their last argument before she discovered him cheating on her.

"It doesn't feel like you need me. More like I'm constantly chasing after you to get your attention. You're always so busy with your blasted job. I want a girlfriend who puts me first."

"I'm just starting out in my career, Brad," Brooke *stated as she crossed her arms defensively. "You need to understand I have to put in the extra time and effort now so that when we're ready to have a family, I can take the time it will require."*

"See, there you go again," Brad *said as he ran his finger through his black hair in frustration. "You're always planning and calculating. Everything is so contractual with you. I don't want you to treat our relationship like a hostage negotiation."*

The words stung. Brooke pressed her lips together and pushed back the tears that threatened to fall. "I'm sorry I make you feel that way. I want to make this work. I love you, Brad."

When he didn't say the words back, she should have seen the writing on the wall; their relationship was doomed. Instead, she had pushed through, pretending they would get through the rough patch.

It wasn't until her friend called her and told her she saw him going into the lobby of a hotel with another woman that Brooke knew it was over. Yet, she had driven the short distance to the Boulder Inn to verify it with her own eyes.

When she entered the restaurant, and saw them holding hands just as he leaned in for a kiss, her heart broke in half. She didn't even have the strength to confront him. Instead, she turned around and walked out the door. She sent him a text via phone telling him she knew what he was doing and to never contact her again.

She hadn't dated, or even looked at another man, until Liam today. When he held her in his arms and she looked up into his hazel eyes, something that had been frozen in her heart thawed. She realized she didn't want to be alone anymore.

"That's what you're wearing?" Trina asked with an arched eyebrow as she came into the common area wearing a form-fitting red dress. "I thought you would at least dress up for dinner."

"I'm wearing slacks, aren't I? I usually just wear jeans."

"She's got you there, Trina," Kristen said with a smirk as she joined them. "That's about as dressy as it will get with Brooke. I, on the other hand, wanted to do it up too."

Kristen was wearing a white dress with tiny rhinestones sewn at the neckline and waist.

Trina made a 'humph' sound under her breath, then said, "We need to get going, our reservation is in ten minutes."

Brooke shrugged. "I wasn't the one who was taking extra time to get ready."

"But wasn't it worth it," Trina said as she spun around in her red mini dress.

"Wow, think much of yourself, do you?" Kristen jabbed.

"Okay, you guys, let's just go eat," Brooke suggested, trying to be the peacemaker between the competitive friends. "I'm tired and my bed is calling me."

The friends made their way to the front door that led to the hall. As they made their way to the elevators, a loud shattering noise filled the area. The trio swung to the right to find a tree had fallen through the window at the end of the hall.

Cold air gusted in, causing the women to shiver and tuck their arms in at their chests.

"We need to tell the management what happened," Brooke declared. "This isn't good. I had no idea this storm would get this bad."

"I don't think anyone did," Kristen stated with a worried look on her face. "Do you think we'll be safe here?"

"Your best friend is a cop. I know just what to do

in this type of circumstance." Brooke glanced at the elevator and shook her head. "We should take the stairs in case the power goes out. We don't want to get trapped in there."

"Agreed," Trina said with a scared look, her fear of tight spaces showing.

The women made their way down the nearby stairwell and entered the main lobby. They reached the front desk, but there was an already growing group of guests complaining about the storm and demanding answers about what to do.

"I want to speak to the manager right now. There is a tree pounding against the wall of my suite. My children can't sleep with that going on," a middle-aged woman was yelling at one of the desk clerks. "You need to find us another room this instant."

"Ma'am, there are no other rooms available. We are filled to capacity."

"That won't do. I refuse to spend another night in that room."

A man in a suit pushed forward and yelled at the mother at the front, "You're complaining about a room? That's not even a real problem." He turned his attention to the clerk. "I have to get back to Denver this evening for a work event. My phone alerted me that the roads are closed due to the storm. How am I supposed to get back?"

"Sir, we can't control the road closures. The police closed them for public safety."

The man let out a long run of curse words before he bellowed, "I don't care what you have to do; I need you to get me out of here."

Brooke had enough of watching everyone bulldoze over the workers of the resort. She put her fingers between her lips and whistled. Everyone turned to face her, their eyes boring into her with angry stares.

"That's enough," she stated curtly. "You all need to calm down and head back to your rooms."

"Who do you think you are?" the businessman asked as he moved towards her in a menacing manner.

Pulling out her badge from her back pocket and holding it up, she announced, "I'm a police officer, so do what I tell you before I put you in handcuffs. The worst thing anyone can do in a situation like this is get upset. We all just need to stay calm."

Everyone backed up as they gave wary glances towards her. As Brooke and her friends moved to the front desk, Kristen leaned over and asked in a hushed tone, "You don't really have handcuffs on you, do you?"

Brooke shook her head. "No, not on me. I have

my gun and cuffs back in the room, but they don't need to know that."

"Maybe you should go get them after this," Trina suggested.

"That's probably a good idea," Brooke agreed.

The clerk gave them a grateful smile as she inquired, "I appreciate the help just a moment ago. What can I do for you, officer?"

"I wanted to let you know the storm caused a tree to fall through the west window of the hotel on the second-floor hall. The guests in that area will need to be careful and someone should board it up before this storm gets any worse."

The woman's eyes grew round with shock. "It was only supposed to be a snowfall, nothing more. We didn't prepare for a storm of this magnitude."

"It will be fine," Brooke stated. "You just need to keep everyone from panicking. The best way is to assure them they're safe."

"But are they?" the woman asked in a whisper.

"It's our job to make sure they are," Brooke explained. But just as the words left her lips, the lights flickered for several seconds before they dimmed and extinguished completely.

There were screams from women, cries from children, and a few grunts from people hitting random objects in the dark. After about a minute, emergency lights came on to barely illuminate the area.

Brooke could tell that law and order were hanging on by a thread. If she wasn't careful, chaos would break out. It would be every man for themselves. She needed to help the staff get control of the situation before that happened.

"I'm guessing from the emergency lights, there are generators somewhere on the property?" Brooke inquired.

The clerk nodded her head. "Yes, we have two. One supplies the power to the lodge common areas while the other provides power to the rooms."

"How long do they have?"

The woman frowned. "I'm not sure, but my guess is not much more than a day or two if we are running power to all areas. The owners planned to upgrade them after the renovation last year, but they never got around to it."

"That's not good. This storm could last longer than that." Brooke thought about their options. An idea came to her. "What if we shut down the power to the rooms and have everyone come in here until the storm passes?"

The woman shook her head. "There's no way the guests would go for that. They wouldn't want to give up their rooms."

"They would if it was their only option," Kristen chimed in. "Tell them it's the only way to insure everyone will stay safe until the storm passes. Tell them about the tree coming through the window and how more could follow. The lobby and lounge area is the only part of the property where everyone can be kept safe."

"That's true," the manager agreed, coming up beside them. "I just oversaw the evacuation of all the cabins. I brought those guests back here. I will make an announcement to everyone what we have to do to survive this storm."

Brooke braced herself for a long night. She would not feel the comfort of a bed anytime soon.

FOUR

A shiver shot up Liam's back as he put the final blanket on his horses. Normally, he didn't put blankets on them when they were in their stalls, but with the freezing temperatures, he worried they would need the extra protection from the biting cold.

He checked their automatic feeders to make sure they had plenty of hay to last through the next couple of days just in case he got snowed in and couldn't get out of his cabin next to the barn. It hadn't happened yet, but this storm was the worst he'd encountered since moving to Colorado.

"How are you doing, girl? You all right, Tinker?" Liam asked as he rubbed the neck of his favorite mare. She was the first horse he'd purchased, and therefore held a special place in his heart.

Tinker neighed in response and pushed her muzzle towards him affectionately.

"I'm going to take off to get some gas from town to make sure we have enough for whatever is coming this way. The generators are ready if we need them, but I'm worried I don't have enough to wait out a massive storm." He moved out of Tinker's stall and latched it shut behind him. He turned to face the four horses and added, "I'll be back soon and will check in on you guys before I settle in for the night."

Liam exited the barn and headed towards his 4-wheel drive Bronco SUV. He jumped up inside and turned on the heater, wanting to warm himself as he drove into town.

It was well below freezing. He was glad he had invested in generators for power outages along with all the needed supplies to shelter his horses in the worst of winter weather. He had, however, used up an extra amount of gas for some projects and worried he wouldn't have enough if he got snowed in for a long period.

The visibility was awful as Liam continued down the road that led to the resort and then town. He could barely make out what was in front of him and leaned forward to make sure he could see the road. The solid yellow line that marked the small road was covered in snow. It was becoming increasingly difficult to push through the white powder.

The turn off for the resort came into view and he realized he needed to change his plans. Perhaps, there would be some spare gas they could loan him so he could make it back to his place before it got any worse. It was bordering on a white-out as he pulled into the driveway that led to the lodge.

Something was off as he approached the employee parking area. The lights were off for the entire area and the place was eerily still. *What is going on? Even with the storm, there should be some activity?*

As Liam exited his car, a sharp blast of icy wind slapped him across the face. His teeth instantly chattered, and his body shook. He pushed forward, trudging through the snow that was piling higher and higher by the second. He moved carefully, unable to see in front of him.

Liam found a wall and inched along it until he found a handle. He pushed forward, releasing the door from its frame, then spilled into the room, causing everyone's eyes to fix on him.

Two of the resort workers rushed over to help shove the door shut. The younger of the two, Buck, asked, "What are you doing here, Liam?"

"I needed to see if the resort had any spare gas I

could borrow. I couldn't make it to town and figured I would check here."

The older grey-haired worker, George, shook his head. "The power is already out here. We're running on backup generators as is. We have no spare gas as we already have had to shut down the generator to the rooms to conserve what gas we have. Everyone is staying in the main common areas of the lodge until the storm passes."

"I guess I need to get out of here and head home then," Liam said, putting his hand on the door handle. "Hopefully, the gas I have there is enough to last until I can get into town in a couple of days."

"No way, Liam. You can't go back out in this," Buck argued. "You won't make it home."

"I agree with him. You need to stay here and wait out the storm," a familiar feminine voice said from behind them.

Liam whipped around to find Brooke only a couple of feet away. She looked good in a pair of black slacks and red sweater which enhanced her natural beauty. Her blonde hair was pulled back in a ponytail—just like the last time he saw her—but his mind strayed to the thought of what it would feel like to pull her hair free and run his fingers through it.

A wave of guilt cascaded over him. He shouldn't even be thinking about her that way, yet every time he was around her, he felt an attraction he couldn't explain.

"I've seen many people get stuck because they think they can navigate a storm. Instead, they end up in a snowdrift never to be found until after the snow melts, and it's too late to save them." She gave him a weary smile. "I wouldn't want that to happen to you."

"Though I appreciate your concern, this isn't my first winter in Colorado. I'll be fine," Liam said defensively, not wanting to give up his man-card.

"The magnitude of this winter storm has taken all of us by surprise. You shouldn't go out there, Liam," George stated. "It's too dangerous."

As if on cue, a loud howl of the wind slammed against the building, causing it to shudder. Though the storm shutters were secure over the windows, it didn't keep the rest of the place from shaking from the raging winds.

The manager for the hotel came into the middle of the lobby and addressed the crowd of approximately a hundred guests. "May I have everyone's attention," he said in a loud authoritative voice. "My name is Donald Brand, and I want to assure all of you we are doing everything we can to keep everyone safe. I just heard over the radio that the storm has been upgraded to a blizzard. Authorities have told everyone to shelter in place and wait it out."

There were many gasps of dismay, murmurings of discontent, and a few cries from children.

"How long are we going to be stuck here?" a man shouted in anger from across the room.

"Are we going to be allowed back in our rooms? I don't want to spend countless hours with a bunch of strangers," a woman near Donald whined. "It's inhuman to deny us access to a bed and shower."

"I don't want to stay here, Mommy!" a little boy screamed at the top of his lungs and stomped his feet. "I want to go home."

"Me too, son, me too," the mother said as she patted the back of the boy.

"Everyone needs to calm down. We *will* be fine. The owners upgraded the property a few years ago with storm shelter features. We will be safe here," Donald assured everyone.

"Oh, really?" another man asked sarcastically from the middle of the crowd. "Then why isn't there enough power from the generators to run the entire lodge? Why did you shut down the power to the guest rooms?"

"We did that to make sure we have enough power to last the duration of the storm," the manager explained. "We don't want to run out so we are conserving it."

"Well, I don't care. I paid a huge amount of money to be here and I want to go to my room," the whiny woman stated in a huff.

"The resort will refund everyone their cost or offer them a complimentary stay once the storm has passed," the manager offered. "We can't do anything about the situation right now except try to tough it out together."

"That's not good enough," the woman fumed. "I want to speak to the owners. Why aren't they here taking care of this? I'm going to leave a nasty review about this experience. I think—"

"All right, that's enough!" Brooke shouted above the whiny woman's complaining. "You heard what the manager had to say. We all need to stay calm."

"And why do you think you have any authority in this situation?" one man nearby questioned Brooke with irritation.

"Because I'm a police officer, and I deal with situations like this all the time. Arguing and complaining won't help," she explained.

"Just because you're some out-of-town cop

doesn't give you the right to come in here and try to tell us all what to do."

"Actually, it does," the manager explained. "Clear Mountain is in Boulder County and her jurisdiction is for all the area. What she says goes."

The man grunted under his breath but didn't argue further. Instead, he turned and slinked off to a corner of the lobby. The rest of the crowd dispersed, leaving Brooke alone with Donald and Liam.

"I'm glad I have my gun and handcuffs on me," Brooke stated. "I hope we won't need either of them, but if people panic and act out, we might end up requiring both."

The manager nodded. "I will let everyone know we will turn the generator on for that area for a short time so guests can gather their belongings and bring them here. Once they have, we'll turn the generator off and keep the gas in reserve to use as needed if the supply for here runs out."

"Is there anything I can do to help?" Liam asked, wanting to assist in any way possible.

"No, just wait with everyone else," Donald stated with a weary grin. "Thank you for the offer though," he added before heading off to work.

"Could you use some company?" Liam inquired.

Brooke nodded. "Sure, you can join my friends and me, if you would like."

They made their way over to her friends sitting on one of the nearby sofas. Liam took a seat in one of the winged-back chairs and settled in for a long night.

FIVE

"I see you found our sleigh driver," Kristen observed.

"Got stuck here like the rest of us, did you," Trina stated. Giving her friend and Liam a knowing smile, she added, "At least you get to hang out with Brooke some more."

Brooke tried to avoid the obviousness of her friends. Why were they always pushing her to find a new guy? It frustrated her that they couldn't understand she didn't want to get hurt again.

She glanced at Liam out of the corner of her eye. What was bothering her the most was the fact she wanted to get to know Liam. There was something about him that drew her in.

"Well, I need to head to the restroom," Kristen said. "Why don't you come with me, Trina."

The women got up from the sofa, and Trina pointed to a stack of board games. "You guys should play a game together to pass the time."

Brooke's friends exited the area and headed towards the hall where the public bathrooms were located, leaving Brooke to figure out what to do with Liam. She glanced down at the board games and decided a game wouldn't be the worst idea.

"So, are you a Dominos or Scrabble guy?" Brooke inquired.

He shrugged. "My family didn't play board games while I was growing up. I think I played Scrabble once at school, so let's try that game."

"I didn't get to play them when I was young either," Brooke admitted as she picked up the box and gestured towards the nearby café. "There are a few tables in there with two chairs. It's also a little quieter."

"Sounds good," Liam said as they made their way into the nearby area.

Once inside, they found a table in a corner and took seats across from each other. Brooke took off the lid to the box and pulled out the game board. She placed it in the center of the table and handed each of them a wooden letter holder. She put the box on top of the board and started flipping the letter tiles over so they were all facing down.

Liam reached into the box and did the same. Only a couple of tiles were left towards the middle. Both of them moved their hands for the same one, causing their hands to graze for a split second.

A shot of electricity zipped up Brooke's arm as warmth followed close behind. Her eyes darted up to meet Liam's, whose own eyes were staring back at her.

Whatever just happened must have been felt by both of them because he seemed startled. Absent-mindedly, he pressed his lips together as he rubbed his stubbled beard with his free hand.

The gesture drew Brooke's attention to his mouth. She wondered what it would feel like to kiss those lips. They looked appealing, like two soft pillows ready for her to try out.

"Are you all right?" Liam asked, breaking her concentration. "The tiles are all flipped over now, but you keep staring at me."

Brooke's cheeks flamed red with embarrassment. She hadn't realized her interest in him was so plain. She couldn't quite shake the sensation that when she was around him she was off-kilter; a sensation she wasn't used to. She prided herself in staying in control at all times.

"I'm fine. I was just distracted," Brooke said in a tone that she hoped sounded nonchalant. The last thing she wanted was for him to figure out he was the reason she was distracted.

Liam moved the tiles around in the box, then motioned to it. "You pick first."

"We can do it at the same time to make it fair," Brooke suggested.

He gave her a playful smirk as he nodded in agreement. "I'm betting the reason you like things to be fair is because of your job. Being a cop attracts people who like order and justice."

Brooke tilted her head as she thought about it. Was it true? Did her personality dictate the career she chose? She supposed there was validity to his observation. "I guess that's possible," she said as she picked out tiles at the same speed as Liam. "I've always liked things to be equal. Even as a child, I didn't like it when anything was unfair."

"I was the complete opposite, caring more about winning when I was young," Liam revealed. "I played a lot of sports and found my competitive nature. It carried over to when I became a stockbroker. I loved the thrill of getting a great deal and one-upping a competitor."

The information about his past surprised her. From his casual dress of a t-shirt and jeans to his sleigh business, she never would have pegged him as the corporate type.

"How did you end up here running a sleigh business," Brooke probed.

"I left my job as a stockbroker after…" a sadness overtook Liam as he paused for several moments before continuing, "my wife died."

A pang of sympathy filled Brooke's heart as she said, "I'm so sorry, Liam."

He put the letters on his wooden block and moved them around in silence as he stared at them. Finally, after several moments, he whispered, barely loud enough for her to hear, "She was killed in a car wreck by a drowsy driver. The person fell asleep behind the wheel, crashing into her. Neither of them survived."

"That's awful. I can't even imagine losing someone like that. How long has it been?"

"Four years. After it happened, I couldn't stay in New York. I wanted to go somewhere else and be someone else. I bought a car and just drove, ending up in Colorado. Figured it was good as of a place as any, so I bought a local newspaper to look for a job. There was an ad asking for workers on a nearby ranch. They said they would train me, so I applied and got the position. After two years of learning about horses, I decided to venture out on my own and start a business."

"Wow, what a change from what you were doing

before," Brooke stated. "Do you like running your sleigh business as much as being a stockbroker?"

"It's very different, and I didn't realize how trapped in a rat race I was until I was out of it," he said, placing the six-letter word "simple" for 19 points. "I focused so much on making money and having a lavish lifestyle I didn't even think about what it was costing me. My wife wanted children, but I told her not until I made my first million, then it was my second million. She got frustrated with my inability to find satisfaction with what we had. I never felt like I had enough."

Brooke laid out a few tiles, spelling the word "emu," for a triple letter score of 22. "It's not your fault. Society causes us to think we need the expensive car, the big house, and the designer clothes. I grew up in the foster care system until I aged out at eighteen. I still wanted all those things. I floundered around trying to figure out how to get them, but nothing stuck. I was working as a bartender when this off-duty cop came in and saw me break up a fight. He told me I should apply for the police academy. I figured, what the heck. What do I have to lose? It was the best decision I ever made. Not just because I found out that helping others as a cop was my calling in life, but because while I was in the academy, I found God too. I'd been in several homes that had different religions, but it wasn't until I found Jesus that it all clicked into place."

"You're a Christian? I am too," Liam shared. "My wife introduced me to God. When we were first married, we went to church all the time, then I got too busy for that as well. I have so much guilt over how I treated her. The way I took for granted the life she wanted with me. I always assumed she would be there—until she wasn't. If I could go back and do things differently, I would've started a family with her when she asked rather than focusing on money."

"You can't beat yourself up for your past mistakes. All you can do is learn from them and not make them again. If you ask God, He can help you with that."

A frown crossed Liam's face as he hesitated before placing the word, "maze,' on the board for a double score of 21. "I know He can. I've just been too afraid to ask Him. Sometimes, I think I deserve the guilt I feel; like I don't deserve God's forgiveness."

"You're right; you don't. None of us do, but God gives it to us, anyway. All you need to do is ask."

"I know you're right. I've held onto my guilt for too long. Thanks for talking with me about it. I didn't expect to get into this tonight."

She gave him a warm smile. "Don't worry about

it. God wanted us to talk about it. You want me to pray with you about it?"

Liam nodded. "I'm pretty rusty, just so you know."

"God doesn't care," Brooke stated with certainty. "He takes us any way He can get us." She reached out and placed her hand on Liam's, then closed her eyes. "Dear Lord, though the circumstances that brought us to this moment were unexpected, it's obvious this was your purpose. You want Liam to give his guilt over to you and for him to accept your forgiveness. Lord, I pray that You help him do that. In Jesus' name, Amen."

She opened her eyes and asked, "How do you feel?"

"Like a burden has been lifted. Like my heart isn't as heavy."

Brooke nodded. "See, great decision, right?" She glanced down at the board and let out a laugh. "You're going to regret putting that 'z' down." She put 'ebra' after it to form the word, "zebra" for a triple letter score of 42.

"You're fantastic at this game," Liam stated with shock. "I think you tricked me by offering it as an option. You're like a Scrabble shark."

"I have a confession to make. I play Words with Friends online all the time."

He shook his head in defeat. "That explains a lot. I think we should switch to a different game; one I might be able to win."

"Oh, now I see it," Brooke stated with a smirk.

"See what?" Liam asked in confusion.

"That competitive nature you were talking about."

"In my defense, I think anyone would be upset if they found out they were playing Scrabble with the rain-man of Words with Friends."

They both laughed this time. It felt good to have fun with a guy again. She hadn't even known she missed being around a man she was attracted to, but now that she was spending time with Liam, she realized it couldn't have been just any man. It had to be the right one.

"What's so funny?"

Brooke looked up to find the sleazy guy from earlier in the day standing a few feet away. He looked drunk with tussled hair and unfocused red eyes. He moved closer, stumbling along the way. The stale liquor smell that wafted off him confirmed Brooke's suspicions. He was definitely inebriated.

"Are you lost?" Brooke asked. "Don't you have somewhere else to be?"

"No, this is a free country. I can go wherever I want," he slurred out as he leaned in towards her.

"Why can't we be friends? Where are your friends? I want all of us to be friends," he yelled as he threw his arm around her shoulders, causing his hand to dangle across her chest inappropriately.

"Get your hand off me," Brooke growled, as she jumped up and moved away from him.

"What's your problem? I told you, I just want to be friends," he said in an angry voice.

"And I told you, I'm not interested," she stated adamantly. "I have plans. To make it clear, those plans are permanent and they don't include you."

"You are such a shrew. I've never met a pricklier woman." He turned his attention to Liam. "Get out while you can, man. This one is a waste of time." He turned his attention back towards her and added, "All that prettiness wasted on a woman who might as well be a man. You act like a man, you work a job like a man. You sure you don't have the equipment of a man?" he said, reaching out and grabbing her by the arm.

Liam stood to his feet, reached over, and grabbed the guy by the front of his shirt, yanking the drunk towards him. "Don't talk to her that way. As a matter of fact, don't ever even look at her again. If you come near her again, you'll regret it." He released the drunk and moved over to stand next to Brooke. "Now, get out of here."

The man scampered off, stumbling along the way. Once he was gone, Liam turned to Brooke and inquired, "How are you?"

"I could have handled that myself," Brooke asserted.

"I know you could. It doesn't mean you should have to." He reached out and placed his hand on the side of her arm. "Did he hurt you?"

"No, it wasn't that bad. I've gotten way worse on the job."

Liam glanced towards the lobby. "I should go tell the manager about that guy. He needs to know what happened and make sure the staff is keeping an eye on him, not to mention cutting him off from anymore alcohol."

"You're right. That guy needs to be locked in a drunk tank, but we don't have access to one with all that is going on with the blizzard."

"We'll figure it out. If he does anything else, you might need to use those cuffs on him."

"Don't tempt me," Brooke stated with a weary chuckle. "It would be my pleasure."

They exited the café and headed back into the lobby, where Brooke joined her friends, and Liam went to find the manager.

SIX

Liam approached the back room behind the front desk. The hotel manager was talking to a couple of the workers. Donald had a worried expression on his face as Liam came up next to him.

"Hey, Donald, I need to give you a heads-up about an intoxicated guest who needs to be watched. He got handsy with another female guest."

"Great, just what I need, one more problem," Donald stated with frustration. "As if having a blizzard shut down everything isn't bad enough, but to have a drunk bothering guests along with guest items disappearing is terrible timing."

"Are you serious? What happened?" Liam asked with concern.

"A guest reported they have money and jewelry missing from their room. If that guest tells anyone, it will create chaos. Guests will panic if they think they're trapped with a thief amongst them. Once they accuse each other, fights will break out. It could get bad really quick."

Liam nodded, worrying what would happen if the truth came out, then an idea came to him. "We have a police officer staying at the resort. What if Brooke Patterson investigates and tries to figure out who took the missing items? If we locate the thief and return the stuff quietly, no one else would need to know."

"You're right, Liam. That's a smart idea. Can you go get Officer Patterson and bring her here?"

Liam nodded and took off for the lobby. He pulled Brooke aside and told her the manager needed to speak with her. A few minutes later, they made their way into the back area.

"Thank you, Officer Patterson, for coming to talk with me. We need your help with a matter that has to be handled as discreetly as possible."

Brooke's eyebrows rose in surprise as she asked, "What is going on?"

"We've had a guest report missing items from their room. The theft happened during the chaos of the power outage. We need you to figure out who took the items and resolve the situation before the guest goes public with what happened. If he does, it could prove dangerous for everyone."

"Can I ask you a few questions?" Brooke asked.

The manager nodded.

"First, where is the room located?"

"On the second floor of the west wing."

"Was it close to the elevator?"

"Hold on. Let me get you a map." Donald grabbed a piece of paper from a drawer along with a pen. He circled places on the map, then handed it over to Brooke. "The star is the lobby, and the circled room is the one that was burglarized."

Brooke studied the map for a few moments, folded it up, and placed it in her jacket pocket. "Do the rooms automatically lock behind them even when the power is out?"

"They're supposed to, but there is a possibility that while the power was coming back online, the rooms were temporarily unlocked. It was an error that our technicians figured out a few months ago. The owners were planning to fix it, but it was going to take a massive overhaul. They were in the process of researching which company to hire to upgrade the electronic key system."

"Was all the staff accounted for during the time of the incidents?"

"I get what you are implying, but I checked with all department heads before involving you. I've cleared everyone on my staff."

"That means it was another guest," Liam observed with disappointment. "It's sad to think some people lack integrity."

The manager nodded. "The question is whether the thief planned to do this or they took the opportunity afforded by the power outage."

"Is there a list of the missing items?"

"Yes, right here," Donald affirmed, as he handed a piece of paper to her.

"All right, I think that is all the information I need for now," Brooke said. "How will I access the room?"

"Once the generators turned on, the doors re-locked; however, we have a master set of traditional keys for the rooms in case the power is ever out," Donald said as he pulled out a ring of keys from his pocket and handed them over to Brooke. "There is a panel below the keycard slot where the key can be inserted."

"Thanks," Brooke said, taking the keyring. "I'll start right away. Can you have someone go tell my friends I'm handling something for the resort please?

I don't want them to worry about me. Also, can you spare a flashlight?"

Donald nodded, taking one from a different desk drawer and handing it to her. "As soon as you have any news, will you let me know?"

"Of course," Brooke said before exiting the back area with Liam following her.

"Why don't I go with you," Liam offered. "I can be an extra set of eyes. Plus, I am familiar with the resort and can help you out."

"Sure, I can use some help; especially if we're going to figure this out quickly." She pulled out the map and glanced down at it, then back up, and pointed towards the west stairwell. "Should we use those stairs to get to the room we need to investigate?"

Liam nodded. "Yes, with the elevators down, that's the quickest way."

They headed towards the door that led to the stairs. As soon as they entered, the darkness settled in. Brooke flicked the switch to the flashlight in her hand while Liam pulled from his pocket a flashlight he'd brought from home.

With both flashlights on, they could see a good distance ahead and navigate the stairwell efficiently.

As they entered the second floor of the west wing

of the lodge, the cold hit Liam with full force, causing him to pull his coat tighter around him.

He glanced over at Brooke to see how she was doing since she only had a sweater on. "Are you all right?"

"What?" Brooke mumbled, distracted as she looked from the room numbers to the map and back up again.

"Are you warm enough? It's freezing in here without the heat on."

She shrugged. "It's chilly, but I'll manage. I've had to work some pretty cold nights while on the graveyard shift in Boulder."

"Yes, but I'm betting you had a coat on when you did," he gestured to her outfit. "Though you look great, I'm not sure what you're wearing will keep you warm."

"I'll be fine. I'm tougher than I look."

"Okay, but if you change your mind, I can give you my coat."

She looked over at him with a frown. "Then won't you and I just switch spots? You'll be freezing instead of me."

"I wouldn't mind if it was a way of making sure you're doing all right."

Her frown turned to a tentative smile. "That's

sweet, and I appreciate the sentiment, but don't worry about me. Besides," she gestured with her head towards the nearby door, "we're at the room that was burglarized. Let's focus on figuring out who took the missing items."

SEVEN

Brooke moved the cover on the door and slipped the key into the lock. She turned the handle and stepped inside, holding it open for Liam until he came into the room.

A quick scan of the area revealed nothing was out of place. It was possible the occupant of the room moved items around and straightened up before telling the manager what had happened.

Brooke moved further into the space, inspecting the area to see if anything stood out to her. She flashed her light on different spots in the room to make sure nothing stuck out as unusual.

She read the list of missing items: a Rolex, five hundred dollars, and a gold ring. The manager noted the items had been in a small bag inside the nightstand.

A glance at the bed confirmed there were two of them. She would have to check both since the note didn't say which one held the items before someone took them. Brooke moved to the closer of the two—the right one—and looked on top, around the edges and underneath. *Nothing. Maybe something inside the drawer will give me a clue.* Disappointment seized her heart when she opened the compartment, shuffled items around, and didn't find anything unusual.

Brooke moved around the bed to the other side. She inspected the second nightstand like the previous one, not finding anything to help her figure out who was responsible for the theft. She turned away and wondered how she would figure out who did it, when something on the ground caught her eye. As she bent down, she focused her flashlight on the spot.

"What did you find?" Liam asked, coming up next to her.

"I think I found a clue," she stated.

A muddy shoe print was partially visible under the edge of the bed. She glanced backwards from it and noticed there were several more, all the way back to the door. Some were smeared while others were partial. There were enough, however, to make it clear someone had been outside before coming into the room. Whoever left the shoe prints must have not realized it happened when they were in the dark. If it was a thief rather than the occupant of the room, then she had a tangible clue to help her find the suspect.

She pulled out her phone and took several pictures of the best ones, knowing she would not only need them for proof, but in order to identify who had been in the room.

"What are you doing?"

"I need these for evidence," Brooke explained. "Plus, I can use them to figure out who was in this room. If the room's occupant never went outside, it eliminates him from being the culprit which means it was the thief."

Brooke took one last look around the room, noting she saw nothing else that would be helpful in her investigation.

"I don't understand how that will help us find who stole the items," Liam confessed.

"I can investigate and see who has muddy shoes. I'm fairly certain not too many people were outside before the storm hit. Then, I can question those who do have mud on their shoes, and by their responses, I'm sure I can figure out who did it."

"Really? That's amazing you can figure that out from a simple muddy shoe print," Liam stated with admiration. "You must be great at your job."

"I have always liked figuring out puzzles ever

since I was a little girl. I am hoping to apply for a detective spot soon. Even though this is less than ideal circumstances, I'm glad for the opportunity to test my observation skills."

They left the hotel room and made their way back through the dark hallway and stairwell to the front lobby.

As Brooke glanced around the lobby, she noted everyone seemed tired and on edge. It was difficult to be stuck with a bunch of strangers, let alone with a blizzard outside and limited resources to share.

She processed the room, eliminating potential suspects. The shoe print was definitely male, which meant all the women and children were out of the question. There were several men sitting with their families, which didn't rule them out, but she could circle back to them if she needed to after her initial group of suspects. There was a cluster of men by the fireplace, another inside the café, and a couple of single men spread throughout the main areas of the lodge.

"Do you want to head over to the fire and warm up?" Liam asked with a concerned expression on his face. "You look so pale."

Brooke glanced over and noticed her friends were talking to the men near the fire. That would give her a good excuse to join them.

"Sure, we can start there. There's a few men nearby I want to check out more closely."

"If I didn't know what you meant by that statement, I think I'd be jealous," Liam said with a smirk. "I don't like the idea of you checking out other guys."

Brooke felt herself blush, not used to men paying that sort of attention to her. Usually, most men she ended up coming in contact with were on the wrong side of a pair of handcuffs. They either had one of two reactions: offended a woman would have the audacity to arrest them, or simply she was incompetent because she was a woman. Neither reaction set well with her.

The only other men she spent time with were work colleagues and they treated her like an outsider because of her gender. She only had two co-workers that were halfway decent towards her. The rest were either condescending or disrespectful, and the worst were a combination of both.

Liam didn't treat her that way. He seemed to not only be okay with her career choice, but respected her for it. A welcome change compared to all the other men in her life.

She glanced over at the athletic, vain group of men, including the annoying drunk from earlier, and felt her stomach tighten with dread. She had no desire to go near them, but knew she had to in order to get her investigation done. "Don't worry. I'm not interested in any of those guys, anyway. They're the opposite type of guy I'm attracted to."

"That's great news, because I'm nothing like them."

Brooke let out a small laugh as she reached out and squeezed his bicep. "Really? You don't seem too flabby and you definitely dress well."

"Hey, I won't argue I attempt to be presentable and to keep up my health, but don't lump me with those imbeciles."

Sobering for a moment, she leaned towards him and whispered, "Don't worry. I'm good at reading people, and I can tell you're a good guy."

A look of appreciation crossed his face as he said, "Thank you. It means a lot to hear you say that."

"From the moment we met when you caught me, to right now while you're helping me track down the thief, you've always put everyone around you first."

There was a burst of loud laughter from across the room, drawing both of their attention to the set of chairs and sofas by the fireplace. The men were pushing each other around and being stupid, trying to evoke reactions from Kristen and Trina, who seemed annoyed rather than amused.

Brooke, followed by Liam, walked over and

joined her friends on the sofa. They both turned their attention to her. Trina asked, "So you're going to tell us your super-secret assignment given to you by the staff here at the resort?"

Deciding to hint at what was going on without revealing too much, Brooke answered loud enough for the men nearby to hear. "Oh, there was a matter that they needed me to investigate. They wanted a cop to handle it and I'm the only police presence right now."

"Can you be any vaguer," Kristen stated as her face scrunched up with irritation. "Leave it to you to always keep us guessing about what is going on."

"Sorry, I'm not at liberty to discuss the details," she said, glancing around at each of the men to gage their reactions, "but let's just say, whoever is involved is in real trouble."

Most of the men looked confused, but the shortest guy in the group looked worried. She didn't recognize the brown-haired man, but as soon as she looked his way, he averted his brown eyes.

Brooke glanced down at his shoes. *No mud and they're too small. It wasn't him, but then why is he so nervous? Does he know something?*

"Well, I'm not sure what's going on, but I'm glad you're handling it," Kristen said with a grateful smile. "You always know what to do."

"I guess it's all the excellent training I received at the Boulder County Police Academy," Brooke said with a smile, "When I get the whiff of something amiss, I won't stop until I figure out the truth."

The nervous guy turned pale as he shoved his hands into his pockets. After a moment's hesitation, he slinked away and headed across the room.

Brooke watched as he joined another man leaning against a wall. The nervous man was talking animatedly to him. They both glanced over at her a couple of times while they conversed.

She looked at the other man's shoes. They were definitely the right size, and they had remnants of mud on them. *Got you,* Brooke thought with conviction. *That has to be the guy who did it.*

Brooke jumped to her feet and moved towards where the two men were standing.

The second man pushed off the wall, shoved his hand through his hair, and rushed from the lobby towards the café.

"Wait for me," she heard Liam say behind her, but she had no intention of waiting.

She continued to sprint across the room. As she entered the café, she scanned the area for the suspect.

That's odd. Where is he? Brooke pondered,

wondering where the man had disappeared to so quickly.

"What are we doing in here?" Liam asked, standing next to her.

"I'm looking for the guy who just came in, but I can't figure out where he's at."

"We can split up and search for him. What does he look like?"

"He looks like that," she said, pointing to a black-haired man wearing a grey t-shirt. "Hey, I need to speak with you," Brooke declared as she moved across the room to where the guy was pushing on windows and then the patio doors, trying to get out of the café.

"He's not getting out through there," Liam explained. "The staff shuttered all the outer windows and doors before the blizzard hit."

The closer Brooke got to him, the more the other man panicked. His eyes were round like saucers and he was sweating with fright.

"There's nowhere to go. You need to stop right now," Brooke said with her authoritative cop voice.

He stopped moving and turned to face them directly. "What do you want? Can't a man have a moment alone around here?"

"If you haven't noticed, we're all trapped in here

together," Brooke pointed out. "Not a lot of space for solitude."

"Exactly, which is why I was just trying to get some fresh air," he said defensively.

"In below freezing temperatures with a blizzard raging outside?" Liam asked with disbelief. "You should come up with a better lie than that."

"Besides, your shoes," Brooke said, gesturing to his feet, "tell me you've already been outside recently. My guess is, it was right before you burglarized Room 223."

"I don't know what you're talking about," the man stated as he narrowed his green eyes, then tried to push past her.

Liam moved over and blocked the man's escape path through the café. "Oh no you don't."

The other man growled at Liam. "Get out of my way."

"No, I think I'm good just like this," Liam said through clenched teeth. "Officer Patterson isn't finished yet."

"Right," he said, giving a dirty look to Brooke, "my friend mentioned some rookie cop was poking around putting her nose in matters that don't concern her. Something to do with stolen items from a room."

I've got you. I just need to keep him talking, and he'll end up talking himself straight into a full confession.

"Wow, your friend sure does know a lot. Tell me, what items were stolen?"

"I heard some money and jewelry, but it all belonged to some uppity businessman. He'll just file some insurance claim and get all of his money back, anyway."

Brooke pulled out her handcuffs. "Mister, you're under arrest for the burglary of Clear Mountain Resort." She stretched out her hand to grab his wrist as she continued. "You have a right to remain silent. Anything you say may be used against you in a court of law."

The man yanked free from her grasp, saying, "Whoa, wait a minute. What are you doing? You've got the wrong guy. I told you it was my friend I was just talking to."

Brooke shook her head. "No, that won't fly with me. You didn't pay attention when you committed the crime and left behind your muddy shoe prints. I'm betting your friend was the watchman while you went into the room. He'll be under arrest too, but for now, I need to finish reading you your rights." She started back into his Miranda Rights as she placed a handcuff on one of his wrists behind his back. "You may consult with an attorney before speaking to the police and the right to have an attorney present during questioning now or in the future. If you can't afford an attorney, one will—"

Before she could finish reciting the rest of the speech and secure the second cuff on his other wrist, the man pushed hard against her, causing her to lose her grip on him. Once he was free, the man took off running towards the exit.

"Stop right there," Brooke shouted as she ran after him. "You're resisting arrest which makes this even worse for you."

The man didn't comply, but instead ran to the exit. He darted past everyone in the lobby and towards the front doors. He pulled on them frantically, but they wouldn't budge.

Brooke came up behind the suspect and reached out to grab him. He moved away just before her hand could grab ahold.

The man pulled his arm back to take a swing at Brooke. Her martial arts training kicked in, and she jerked back and ducked out of the way, putting her own hands up in defense.

The suspect struck out at her again. This time she blocked his attack with the side of her arm, and then countered it with a strike of her own, which landed squarely on his chest. She followed it by a leg sweep that dropped the man to the floor. He was writhing in pain when Brooke moved over to stand above him.

"I told you not to run. Next time you'll listen when someone tells you to do something." She flipped him over onto his stomach and secured the cuffs on his wrists behind his back, patted him down, pulled out his wallet and looked at his name, then finished reading him the rest of his rights.

Somewhere amid her securing the subject, the manager for the resort showed up next to them along with several of the guests.

Donald leaned towards Brooke and whispered, "This was exactly what I was trying to avoid. Now everyone will be asking what happened."

"Tell them there was an incident at the hotel, but it's under control thanks to Officer Patterson," Liam said as he joined them.

"It's almost under control," Brooke corrected, "but there's still one more loose end. Before I can handle that, I need to make sure this guy is out of commission until the police can show up and take him into custody."

Brooke walked the suspect over to the lounge and secured his cuffs to a metal pole that ran along the edge of the bar. She pointed to a barstool and ordered, "Don't move from that spot."

The man nodded his head while keeping his eyes

averted. He reminded her of a whipped puppy, the way he was behaving.

As she moved towards the exit of the lounge, the manager asked, "What else do you have to do?"

"I've got to go arrest his accomplice." Realizing she didn't have another set of handcuffs, she asked, "Do you have any zip-ties around here?"

The manager nodded. "We have some in the back room. Let me get you a few."

A few minutes later, he arrived with a handful. "What do you need them for?"

"They work as handcuffs in a pinch," Brooke explained as she put them into the pocket of her pants.

Once she had everything she needed for the second arrest, she scanned the area. The nervous man wasn't present. *Where did he get off to? There aren't a lot of options. Maybe his friends know.*

Brooke made her way over to the group of guys who had taken their place back by the fireplace after all the craziness of the arrest. They all eyed her with suspicion as she approached. One of them blurted out with irritation, "Come to hassle a few more unsuspecting guests?"

She shook her head. "No, I'm just here to right a few wrongs. Where's your friend?"

"You mean besides the one you arrested and

chained in the lounge like an animal?" a second man asked with sarcasm.

"How well do you know your *friends*?" Brooke inquired. "Not well, I'm guessing, since both are thieves. If you know where the other one went, and you don't tell me, that makes you an accomplice. I can put all of you under arrest."

"I don't think you have enough handcuffs for that," the first man said, stepping menacingly towards her.

"No, but she's got plenty of zip-ties, a mean left hook, and me," Liam said, stepping forward and putting his body between them.

"To heck with this, we barely know those two guys. We met them here when we arrived a couple of days ago. We don't owe them any loyalty," a third man in the group interjected. "When you chased after Vince in the café, Doug took off. He mumbled something about heading to his room."

"Thank you for telling me," Brooke stated as she turned to leave to go find the other man.

"Wait up, I'm coming with you," Liam said as he joined her.

"You don't need to," Brooke countered.

"No way. I've gone this far with you, I want to see it through to the end." Then reaching out, he took her hand and added, "Besides, I wouldn't want anything to happen to you."

Warmth spread up her arm from where his hand touched her own. It wasn't only his closeness that made her feel good, it was the affection behind his words.

"I guess you're right. You've proven yourself a great partner tonight. I'll take you as backup anytime."

Brooke found the manager and asked what room the man was staying in. It turned out he was staying only a few doors down from the room they robbed. It made sense they targeted a room nearby. It would provide a plausible cover why they were there if anyone had stumbled upon them as they were entering or exiting the room, or noticed Doug standing outside the room while Vince robbed it.

Liam and Brooke headed back through the stairwell and up to the second floor. They made their way down the hall to room 219.

She still had the key to the room, but as she pulled it out and slipped it into the lock, her cop instincts made her stop before entering. She pulled out her handgun, raising it in preparation to enter the room.

"What's wrong?" Liam inquired.

Brooke raised her hand and placed her index

finger towards her lips, the gesture telling Liam to be quiet. He nodded in understanding as she pressed the tactical light on her gun, then pushed the door open.

They entered the hotel room and stopped just past the threshold, both scanning the area with their flashlights.

Brooke's light landed on the nervous, short man in the corner of the room. He was placing items into a duffle bag and paused with a shocked expression on his face.

"Put your hands in the air, right now," Brooke commanded.

"What… what do you want?" the other man stammered out.

"Doug Lomac, you're under arrest for aiding Vince Sturgess in the robbery of Clear Mountain Resort," Brooke declared.

"I didn't have anything to do with that," the man stated adamantly.

She noticed his right hand wasn't coming out of the bag and warning bells sounded in her head. "I told you to get your hands up where I can see them."

"And I told you, you've got the wrong guy," he countered, still not taking his hand out of the bag.

"We'll let a jury sort that out when you have your

day in court. In the meantime, you're coming with me."

"I don't think so," Doug said as he whipped out a gun from his bag and pointed it at Brooke.

"Don't be foolish, Doug. You don't want to do this," Liam stated, drawing the other man's attention towards him.

"Shut up. You don't know what I want. I can't believe I let that idiot, Vince, talk me into helping him."

"It sounds like he really messed you over," Liam agreed, "but you can return the favor by telling us what happened."

"It was all his idea. He noticed our door unlocked when the power went out. Room 223 was the first one without guests he came upon during the time of the outage."

Brooke moved towards Doug while he was focused on Liam. She was grateful for the distraction and suspected it was the reason Liam continued to keep him talking.

As soon as she was close enough, Brooke lunged towards Doug and the gun in his hand. His finger must have been on the trigger because a shot rang out right before she knocked the gun from his hand. She tackled him to the ground and wrestled with him until she could subdue him after landing several hard blows to his abdomen and face. She pulled out the zip-ties from her pocket, secured his hands behind his back, then moved him over to a chair.

"Don't move," she ordered as she leaned over and picked up the suspect's gun.

Brooke turned to check on Liam. She knew something was wrong the moment her eyes locked with Liam's. His face was white, and he was holding his shoulder.

"Did he hit you?" Brooke asked with concern.

"I think so," he said with shock.

She rushed to Liam's side, worried the damage was extensive. Once beside him, she pulled his hand back and looked.

"Oh, thank goodness," she said, letting out a heavy sigh. "He nicked you. It won't even require stitches."

Brooke darted into the nearby bathroom and grabbed a hand towel from the shelf. She pressed it against the wound, saying, "You need to keep this firmly against it while we head downstairs with Doug over here. The manager will have a first aid kit and I can patch you up as soon as he is secure."

Liam nodded. "Thank you."

"You shouldn't be thanking me," she said, giving him a wry smile. "You took a bullet because you came with me."

"Like you said, it's only a scratch. I'll be fine," he stated, taking over pressing the towel to his wound. As he did, his hand grazed hers, causing a tingling sensation to shoot up Brooke's arm. Her eyes met his and she could see he felt the connection as much as she did.

"I'm glad you are all right," Brooke whispered. "You had me worried."

"I'm glad to hear you care enough to worry," he said, tilting his head, so it came closer to her.

"What can I say, you've grown on me," she admitted, leaning towards him, only stopping a few inches away from his face.

The tension between them was palpable. Her eyes drifted to his mouth, and she wondered what it would feel like to kiss him.

Groans of pain interrupted the moment, drawing Brooke's gaze over to Doug. "We need to get downstairs."

"Agreed," Liam said, standing to his feet.

Brooke moved over and retrieved the suspect. They headed out of the room and back down to the lobby.

EIGHT

Relief flooded Liam once the blizzard passed, and they could call for local police support. Clear Mountain cops arrived to take the suspects into custody. During their interview of Doug, he confessed and divulged they hid the money and jewelry in Vince's room. The officers searched the room and found the stolen items, confirming that they were the thieves.

Brooke and Liam were waiting in the corner of the café for the on-site investigation to wrap up.

"How are you feeling?" Brooke asked, as she eyed him, touching his shoulder.

"It hurts, but I'll be okay," he said as he gingerly rotated his arm.

"I'm glad it wasn't worse. I only have basic first aid training."

"You did a great job of patching me up."

"She sure did," Clear Mountain K-9 Officer Zach Turner agreed, with his dog Harley beside him.

"Not to mention, figuring out who was responsible for stealing the items from the hotel room," fellow K-9 Officer Aiden O'Connell stated as he joined them with his dog Cooper. "You did a great job, Officer Patterson. You should be proud of yourself."

"We just had an officer move away, leaving an opening at our substation. You should apply for the position," Zach suggested. Giving her a flirtatious smile, he added, "We could use a little more feminine charm on the Clear Mountain team."

Liam immediately went from being grateful for Zach's presence to wishing he would go away. His eyes narrowed, and he stiffened with irritation at the officer's crassness.

Not only was it disrespectful to talk to Brooke that way, Liam didn't like another man flirting with her in front of him. *No way am I letting this guy swoop in and hit on Brooke.*

Before Liam could say anything to combat the officer's advances, Brooke shook her head. "Thanks, but I have no desire to transfer to a place that wants me for my 'feminine charms.' Besides, I was planning to test for detective during the next opening. I don't want to transfer to another substation where I end up at the bottom of the pile again."

Liam smiled with satisfaction. He should've figured he didn't need to interject on Brooke's behalf. She was quite capable of defending herself.

"Sorry, meant nothing negative by it," Zach said with a shrug. Turning to his partner, Aiden, he added, "I'll head to the car. Catch up with me when you're ready to take the suspects over to the jail." Zach sauntered off towards the exit of the lodge.

Once he was gone, Aiden turned to face Brooke and Liam. "I'm sorry about my partner. He can't help himself when he's around women. He's not wrong though; there is an opening at our substation. We could use someone with your set of investigative skills. Think about it."

Brooke nodded. "Thanks for the offer. Like I said, I'm happy where I'm at, but it's nice to know there's other options if that should change."

"Sounds good. We have your statement and contact information for any follow-up we might need," Aiden said before he left with his K-9 partner.

Brooke turned to Liam. "I saw your reaction to what Officer Turner said."

"He wasn't being respectful."

"I'm used to dealing with situations like that all

the time. I get treated that way a lot because I'm a female officer."

"Well, you shouldn't have to. You deserve better than that."

A blush tinged Brooke's cheeks pink as she said, "Thank you. It's not often someone sticks up for me." She tilted her head and asked hesitantly, "Was that the only reason he upset you with what he said?"

Should he tell her? He wasn't sure what she would think if he told her the truth. As he looked at her, he realized he wanted her to know how he felt.

"No, it wasn't the only reason. I didn't like his attempt to flirt with you."

"Why?"

"Because I don't want to think about the possibility of you with any other man."

She inhaled sharply as her eyes grew wide with surprise. "Is that so? Then who should I be with, exactly?"

Liam reached out and pulled her towards him. "Me," he whispered, before letting his mouth gently claim her lips in a tender kiss.

Brooke stood still for a moment before she relaxed into his arms, then accepting the kiss and returning it. Her lips and body molded to him, intensifying the passion behind their connection.

"Hmm, hmm," Liam heard from behind them, causing them to end the kiss.

They turned to find Brooke's friends, who were both standing there smiling at them.

"We were coming to tell you, we're heading back to Boulder," Kristen stated. "Our families want us to come home. They were worried about us because of the blizzard. Plus, we're exhausted from all that happened."

"But we think you should stay here and finish the time we booked at the resort," Trina added with a knowing smile. "Besides, you could use the break after all you did to locate those thieves."

Brooke glanced over at Liam, then back at her friends. "I guess that's not the craziest idea."

"We're going to pack up. We'll see you when you get back into town," Kristen reached out and hugged Brooke.

"Have a good time," Trina said, also giving her a hug before they left.

Once they were gone, Brooke turned to Liam and asked, "Are you okay with me staying here for a couple more days?"

"I think that kiss we just shared should tell you I'm more than okay with you staying," Liam stated with a smile. "I love the idea of spending more time with you."

"Glad to hear it, because I'm looking forward to it too."

NINE

Three deep breaths later, and Brooke had her jitters under control. She was excited to see Liam, but wasn't sure how they would do exploring a relationship together. They'd spent little time alone together that wasn't in a high-stress situation. She wondered if they would enjoy each other's company without a blizzard raging outside, or a mysterious crime to solve.

"You ready to go brave one of the Black Diamond runs?" Liam asked as he met Brooke in the lobby of the resort.

"How about we start out on a Blue Square trail first?" she asked with hesitation.

His face wrinkled in confusion. "I'm shocked you asked that. I didn't take you for someone who would shy away from a challenge."

Brooke crossed her arms and shook her head. "I don't, but I haven't skied in two years. Been too busy catching bad guys and protecting the public for any vacation."

"Well, you're getting one now, so I guess we have enough time to start out on some kiddie slopes," Liam teased with a chuckle. "Should we go get in line for the bunny hill?"

"Stop it," she said, letting her own laugh ring out. "I'm not saying we need to go that far. How about we do one blue square then I should be good to tackle the tougher trails?"

Liam reached out and placed his hand on the side of her face. "Sounds like a plan. I can't wait to race you down the mountain."

Her eyebrows shot up with amusement. "I see your competitive side is coming back out."

"I'm pretty laid back most of the time, but when it comes to sports or games, I'm a beast," he said with a smile. "Let's see if you can keep up."

They made their way outside and over to the ski lift. As they reached the top, the mountain was swarming with tourists climbing off the lifts and getting ready to ski down the various slopes.

Brooke pulled down her goggles, bent down with her ski poles at her side, and then looked over at Liam. "You ready to get schooled on these slopes?"

"Oh, you think you're going to school me, do you?" Liam asked in return with a grin. "I don't think so. I'll see you at the bottom," he stated as he pushed off with his own poles and swooshed past her.

"Hey, wait. That's not fair," Brooke shouted after him as she pushed off to chase after him.

Once they were both at the bottom of the hill, they pulled up their goggles and worked at catching their breath.

"That was impressive," Liam admitted. "You not only caught me, but passed me up."

"I told you not to count me out," Brooke stated.

"Clearly, you know exactly what you're doing," he said as he leaned over and placed a peck on her lips. "Did I mention, I enjoyed the view coming down the hill?"

She let out a laugh. "No, but now I'll be self-conscious every time I come down the mountain and you're behind me."

"Don't be. You're perfection."

Brooke's heart fluttered at the compliment. It felt good to have Liam praise her. "Thank you. You're not so bad looking yourself," she said, giving him a quick kiss back. "Let's get up there and take on the Black Diamond trail."

"Lead the way," Liam said as he they headed towards the lifts.

Two runs down the hill later, and the couple decided it was time to take a rest.

"You want to grab some hot cocoa before we get ready for dinner?" Liam asked.

"That sounds delicious," Brooke admitted. "Especially if there is a cookie we can get with it. I'm a sucker for a fresh-baked Snickerdoodle."

"You got it," Liam said as they moved towards the benches to remove their skis before heading to the lodge where the café was located.

When they finished taking off their skis and stood to leave, a skier came barreling down the mountain. The man tried to slow down, but not in time to keep from bumping into Liam, causing him to tumble forward and onto Brooke.

She gasped, shocked by the sudden accident that put Liam on top of her. His strong frame pressed against her softer one, pushing her further into the snow drift. Though the cold surrounded her, the warmth of Liam's body scorched Brooke to the core.

"Are you all right?" Liam inquired with concern as their eyes locked.

Swallowing the lump that had formed in her throat, she murmured, "I'm fine."

"You look beautiful with the snow around you

like that. Like my very own snow angel," Liam whispered as his mouth descended to meet hers.

The kiss was much stronger and demanding than any of the previous ones they shared. She could feel the passion behind it, and let herself melt into it, placing her hands around Liam's neck.

"Are either of you hurt?" she heard a man say from the side, interrupting their kiss. "I couldn't control my speed. I came back here to make sure you're both okay."

"We're good," Liam said as they both scrambled to their feet.

"Glad to hear it." The man tilted his head as if trying to figure something out. Then a moment later he added, "Hey, aren't you the cop who arrested the thieves from the blizzard?"

Brooke nodded. "Yes, that was me."

"I wanted to say thank you. It was awesome of you to do that."

"I was just doing my job," Brooke said, trying to minimize the whole event.

"No way. Few people would have done what you did. You kept all of us safe."

"She's amazing like that," Liam stated with admiration.

Not comfortable with all the attention, Brooke

said, "Thanks for checking on us, but we have to be going."

"Well, take care, Officer, and again, thank you," the man said before taking off towards the lifts.

"It seems I'm dating the resort's new celebrity."

"Not you too," Brooke said with a roll of her eyes. "You shouldn't have encouraged him."

"Why not? You deserve the recognition for what you did."

Still not wanting him to make a big deal about it, she changed the subject by saying, "Let's go get that hot cocoa you promised me. I'm feeling the chill out here."

Liam nodded. "Sure thing," he said, as he gathered their skis and poles from the ground and put them under his arm. He reached out and grabbed Brooke's free hand with his, then guided her to the resort.

TEN

Brooke and Liam separated after their hot cocoa time. He had two guests that had booked a sleigh ride for the afternoon. She needed to check the resort boutique for a dress, considering she didn't bring anything but pants and tops from home.

Just as she was finishing up purchasing the perfect outfit, she heard sirens outside the lodge.

"Do you mind having this delivered to my room?" Brooke asked the sales associate.

"No, not at all," the black-haired woman named Janice stated with a smile. "I'll have it done right away, Officer Patterson."

It figures. Another person who knows me from what happened during the blizzard. Ignoring how uncomfortable the recognition made her, Brooke simply said, "thank you" and left the store.

Once outside, she headed towards the police SUV parked on the side of the resort. Aiden and Zach were getting their dogs out of the back of the vehicle and meeting with the local ski patrol.

"What's going on?" Brooke asked with curiosity as she approached the group.

"We have a report of a missing couple," Aiden explained. "The manager believes they may have snuck out of the lodge right before the storm hit. In all the chaos, no one noticed they were missing, but they were supposed to check out this morning and never did. The manager called the phone number they had on file, but it went straight to voicemail."

"What are you guys going to do?" Brooke inquired.

"Well, Harley and Cooper are trained in search and rescue in winter conditions, so after we let them imprint on a piece of clothing, they hopefully will be able to locate them," Zach expounded.

"Can I come with you? I can be an extra set of hands. I would hate to think I could have helped but didn't."

Aiden and Zach looked at each other for a moment, then both shrugged.

"Sure; if the missing guests are in bad condition, we could use all the help we can get."

Brooke slipped on the extra set of snow shoes they had, along with a police jacket, while Aiden and Zach leaned down and let their dogs smell the sweater of one of the missing persons. Once the K-9s were ready, their handlers gave the command to search.

The dogs took off running, heading towards the outskirts of the resort. Aiden, Zach, and Brooke followed after them, making sure to keep up with the dogs.

Every few yards, the dogs would stop, sniff an area, and then continue on an unseen path only they could follow.

The group came upon the area where four cabins were clustered together. The dogs bypassed the first three structures, but when they reached the furthest one out, the dogs started barking and jumping around.

Though Brooke wasn't a trained K-9 handler, she was aware of their responses from calls she had been on when their assistance was needed. The dogs' reactions meant they had a possible location for the missing couple.

Zach knocked on the door, then said, "Clear Mountain Police. Is anyone in there?"

There was no response from the other side. Zach turned the knob, which was locked.

"We should check the outside to see if they might have gotten in a different way," Aiden suggested. "Why don't you go around on the right side and I'll take the left with Brooke."

"Sounds good, partner," Zach stated as he took off in the direction Aiden designated.

"How long have you and Zach been partners?"

"Around three years now," Aiden said. "He's a great cop and an even better partner. He's always got my back."

"It's good you found someone like that to work with. I'm still trying to find someone like that myself."

"I was serious about that job opening. You should really think about it. I think you would like working with us at Clear Mountain."

Brooke was about to respond when they found a broken window at the side of the cabin. "If they're in there, they probably got in through here."

Aiden and Brooke came around to the back of the cabin where Zach was already waiting by the door.

"Did you find anything?" Zach asked.

"We did," Aiden stated. "There was a broken window on our side."

"I guess that means we need to break the door

down," Zach said, gesturing behind him. "I tried the knob and it's locked too."

"Guess you're right then," Aiden said. "You want to do it, or should I have the honor?"

"I got the last one, your turn," Zach stated.

"Okay. Everyone stand back," Aiden said as he lifted his leg and then kicked out towards the door. His foot made contact with it, causing it to splinter open.

The group entered into the premise. The light from the outside only illuminated the first couple of feet into the space. Both Aiden and Zach flicked on their flashlights, bringing more light into the area.

They scanned the area, finding no one present. They continued further into the cabin where there was a second door. Aiden reached out and opened it.

On the other side were two people huddled together in the bed.

Brooke rushed up to them, worried they hadn't survived due to the below freezing temperatures over the past couple of days. She stretched out her hand and placed it on the first person; a male who was cold to the touch. Though he was unconscious, she could feel a slight pulse.

"The male is alive, but barely," Brooke stated as she pulled him over onto his back. "Do you have a heating blanket? I think he's suffering from hypothermia."

Aiden came over and handed Brooke what she requested.

Zach was working on the female, trying to get her to regain consciousness. "She's not much better," he said, opening a second thermal blanket and wrapping it around her shoulders.

Aiden hit the button on his radio, saying, "Dispatch, this is K-9 2. We've located the missing guests. Both are alive but in critical condition. Can you contact the air unit and direct them to our location for an immediate medical extraction?"

"Copy that, K-9 2," Deanna stated over the radio. "Standby, will update with an estimated time of arrival."

"What else can we do for them?" Brooke asked with concern, as she pulled the blanket tighter around the man.

"We keep them warm, and try to get them to wake up," Zach stated. "If they do regain consciousness, then we should try to get some water in them. They're probably battling dehydration as well."

They worked on getting the couple to respond. The woman started mumbling under her breath. Her words didn't make any sense, but Brooke came over and was able to coax her into taking a sip of water. The man continued to remain unchanged.

"K-9 2, this is Dispatch. We have an arrival time of ten minutes for the air unit. Please have the storm victims ready for departure."

"Copy that, Dispatch. We'll be ready," Aiden stated.

By the time the air unit arrived, they had both of the victims outside, prepared to load. Once the couple was secured in the helicopter and on their way to the hospital, the three of them leaned up against the side of the cabin to take a break.

"Man, that was intense," Zach said as he ran his fingers through his hair. "I'm glad we got them talking before they left. Even though everything they were saying didn't make sense, it means they have a fighting chance."

"True. I can't believe they made it out this far with that blizzard raging." Brooke stated.

"You'd be surprised, all the crazy places we've found people," Aiden stated. "Inside old campers, abandoned factories, even caves sometimes."

"Wow, it's so amazing Harley and Cooper are able to find people considering all that," Brooke stated. "You guys really know what you're doing."

"Thanks," they both said as they pushed off the wall.

"It's time to head back," Zach stated, moving towards the resort. "I want to get back and fill out the paperwork for this. I have a hot date waiting for me at The Lucky Penny."

Aiden rolled his eyes. "Let me guess, another badge bunny." Then glancing at Brooke, he quickly apologized. "I'm sorry. I shouldn't have said that in front of you."

She shook her head. "Don't worry about me. I've heard it all." Glancing over at Zach, she added, "And it's not surprising that's the plans he has for the night."

"And what about you? Aren't you sticking around here because of that sleigh driver fella?" Zach accused.

Brooke stiffened, not liking the comparison. "It's not the same thing at all."

"Really? How long have you known him?" Zach probed.

"Not long, but we've been through a lot in that short time. He's a good guy and we get along well."

"Wow, you sound so clinical when you describe," he gestured to her, asking, "whatever is going on with you and him. What about passion? You can't have a real relationship without it."

Brooke narrowed her eyes. "You don't know what

you're talking about. And for the record, we have plenty of that too."

The moment she said it, she regretted it. There was no way Zach was the type to let a statement like that go.

"Oh, so now it *all* makes sense. He lit a fire that had been dormant all this time," Zach stated with a wag of his eyebrows.

"Ugh, nothing like *that*. We're both Christians." Irritated with Zach's interrogation, she stated, "Can we drop the subject please."

"That's enough, Zach," Aiden chastised. "Leave Brooke alone already." Turning to face her, Aiden stated, "Despite how annoying Zach can be, you should really consider that position at Clear Mountain. This is the second time you've handled yourself well in a high-stress situation. We could use someone like you."

"Thank you. Like I said, I'm not sure what the future holds, but I'll pray about it."

A few minutes later, they arrived back at the lodge. Brooke said her goodbyes to the officers, then headed inside to get ready for her date with Liam.

ELEVEN

Liam waited at the front of the restaurant for Brooke to meet him.

He had gone home, put away his sleigh and horse, changed his outfit, and returned to the resort to treat Brooke to dinner on their first date. At least in his mind it was a date. They hadn't put a label on it or anything, but as far as he was concerned, that was what he considered it.

He squeezed his hands at his side as he looked around the waiting area of the elegant restaurant. The place was warm and glowing with dimmed lights and flickering candles. There were pictures on the wall of the French countryside along with French mottos sprinkled amongst them. The walls were a deep red, accented by soft, gold swirls.

Through the front window, he saw Brooke

approach the restaurant. She looked gorgeous in a black, knee-length dress that was form fitting through the waist and flared out and around her legs. Her blonde hair was down—the first time he had ever seen it that way—and was flouncing around her neck and shoulders as she moved. She was also wearing makeup. Maybe the change in appearance meant she considered this a date too.

Brooke entered the restaurant and made her way over to Liam's side.

"You look beautiful," he said with a grin.

"Thanks," she returned with a smile.

"You ready to try the best restaurant in all of Clear Mountain?"

She nodded. "I've read great reviews about this place. I'm glad I will get to experience it. That whole blizzard thing messed up our plans to eat here the other night."

Liam chuckled. "Well, there isn't a cloud in the sky now. We should be good this time."

He went to place his hand on her back and noticed something out of place. "I don't want to embarrass you, but you have a tag sticking out from your dress."

"Oh no," she gasped, reaching behind her and trying to find it. "I totally forgot to take it off before putting the dress on."

When she couldn't reach it, Liam plucked it from the dress and handed it to her. "Here you go."

"Thank you," she said as her cheeks tinged with pink. "I was in such a hurry after buying it at the resort boutique, it slipped my mind."

"You just bought it?"

She nodded. "I didn't bring anything nice enough for a date. I didn't care enough to impress anyone, at least until now," she admitted before averting her eyes, her face still flush with embarrassment.

He placed his hand under her chin and lifted her face until their eyes met. "First off, you don't need to impress me. That happened a long time ago when I saw you in action during the blizzard. Second, you look good in anything you wear—from your snowsuit, to a pair of jeans and a t-shirt, like the first day we met."

"You remember that?" Brooke asked with surprise.

"I remember everything about our time together."

She replaced her embarrassed expression with one of appreciation. His mouth descended to hers and claimed it with his own. A tender kiss expressed how much he cared about her.

"Everyone is looking at us," she whispered as she pulled back and glanced around the restaurant.

"Let them look," he whispered back, claiming her mouth once more for effect.

After he finished kissing Brooke good and well, he placed his hand on her back and turned to the hostess. "We're ready to be seated."

The woman gave them a friendly smile before guiding them to a table towards the back of the restaurant. They took their seats and both reviewed the menu until the server showed up.

"What can I get you both to drink?" the thin, brown-haired man asked, as he pushed his glasses up off the edge of his nose.

"I'll take a sparkling water," Brooke said.

"And I'll have an iced tea," Liam ordered.

"I'll be right back with your drinks and then will be ready to take your order."

The server disappeared and Liam looked over at Brooke again. "So, a couple of the workers were talking about the missing guests you helped locate today. Seems I wasn't the only one busy working today."

Brooke shrugged. "It was nothing. Aiden and Zach showed up and I offered to help."

"Sounds about right. I only want to know one thing, did Zach hit on you again?'

She laughed as she shook her head. "No, just the

opposite. He mentioned he had a date and then decided to pick apart our relationship."

"I hate to tell you, but the only reason a guy does that is if he's interested in a woman."

"Well, it doesn't matter. I'm not interested in him." She reached across the table and patted Liam's hand. "My attention is completely focused on a handsome sleigh driver."

"Glad to hear it," Liam said with a grin. "So, tell me, how long have you been a cop?"

"Just over five years now. I plan to test for detective the next time a spot opens."

"What does that entail?"

Brooke set down her menu and answered, "I have to take a detailed test, then I'm interviewed by a panel from that department. During the interview, they ask me scenarios to see how I would go about investigating each situation. Once the testing is done, they rank the officers by their scores from both parts."

"Wow, that sounds intense."

"It is, which is why I've waited so long to do it. I am worried I won't measure up."

"You shouldn't count yourself out like that. From what I could tell from the incident during the blizzard, you're a natural."

"Thanks. I hope you're right."

The server showed up with their drinks and a basket of French bread. He placed the items on the table, then asked, "Would you like to start with an appetizer? A salad or soup, perhaps?"

Both of them shook their heads.

"May I start with your main course, ma'am?"

"I'd like to try the duck with potato fingerlings, please," Brooke ordered.

"Superb choice, ma'am." He jotted down the order before turning his attention to Liam. "What can I get you, sir?"

"How about the prime rib with the mixed vegetables and baked potato, please?"

The man nodded as he added the request to the order.

"Enjoy your drinks and bread. I'll be back to check on you," the server said before heading off.

"So, you mentioned what you used to do and how you ended up here in Clear Mountain, but you didn't mention any family. Did you leave anyone behind in New York?"

Liam stiffened under the question, still not happy with the way things were with his family. "I was an only child. My parents didn't like my choice to become a Christian. They didn't approve of my late wife, and blamed her for convincing me to take part in her 'religious nonsense.' The wedge was there before she died. When they came to visit after she passed, they told me I was better off without her because we could go back to how things were before. For this reason, I stopped communicating with them altogether. It was hard, but even after she died, my faith was still important to me. I didn't want to betray Linda's memory."

"I'm sorry they did that to you. I never had a family, so I don't know what it would be like to have them turn on me like that."

Liam could kick himself for making such a big deal about what happened with his parents. "Here I am complaining about my situation with my parents, and you grew up on your own."

"Don't do that; you have a right to be upset with how they treated you. Just because I didn't have parents, doesn't discount the fact of what happened to you."

"Thanks for listening. I've never had anyone—besides God—to talk to about any of this."

"Sure; I want you to feel you can tell me anything," Brooke stated.

"Does it go both ways?" Liam probed. "Can I ask you anything?"

Brooke pressed her lips together as she tilted her head and stared at him. After a moment's hesitation, she answered, "Yes, you've proven I can trust you."

"How are you not in a relationship? You're beautiful, smart, capable. I mean, don't get me wrong, I'm happy you're not because we wouldn't be here right now, but I don't get why."

"It boils down to the fact I'm too capable. My job and independent streak threatened my ex-boyfriend. He said he felt like I didn't need him. He also resented how much time my job took up. I tried to change, honestly I did, but it's not in me to make a man my entire world. Eventually, he ended up cheating, and when I found out, I ended things. That was about a year ago. Ever since the break-up, I've focused on work, not wanting to go down the same road."

"Why did you take a chance on me?"

"Because you're the first guy who seems unintimidated by my job."

"That's because I'm not. I admire what you have chosen to do with your life. It's such a sacrificial job—it's a testament to what type of person you are."

"Stop it. You'll give me a big head," she said with a laugh.

"Not possible."

Their food arrived, and they ate their meal, talking about their jobs, her friends, and the resort. As the meal ended, the server returned with a dessert menu. He handed them each a copy, saying,

"Tonight, we have a decadent cranberry crème brûlée, a specialty of the chef."

Liam glanced over at Brooke. "Are you wanting dessert?"

She shook her head. "Sugar goes right to my hips. I've had enough of it on this trip already. It takes forever to work it off, and I've managed this long to not have to order new uniforms."

Liam handed his menu back and said, "We're good, thanks. Just the check, please."

"The manager told me to let you know there won't be a check. The meal is on the house as a 'thank you' for what Officer Patterson did during the blizzard."

"That's unnecessary. I was doing my job," Brooke objected to the special treatment. "Besides, Liam helped as much as I did."

"All the more reason the meal is on us." the server informed her. "Enjoy the rest of your evening."

Liam pulled out three twenties and placed them on the table. "The meal might be taken care of, but that doesn't mean we can't tip our server."

A few minutes later, they were standing by the elevator that lead to the second floor. Brooke leaned over and pressed the button.

"I had a wonderful time with you today," Liam said as he reached out and placed his hands on the side of her arms. "I was wondering if you wanted to spend tomorrow with me. I could pick you up and I could show you my place. I know it's Christmas Eve, and you might have plans, but I don't want our time together to end."

Her eyelashes fluttered as she looked up into his. "I don't have any real plans. I had a pity invite from Kristen to spend the holidays with her family, but she would understand if I stayed here and spent them with you instead."

"Is that a 'yes' then?" he asked with a hopeful tone.

She nodded as he moved towards her, closing the small gap between them. "I'm glad," he whispered right before he moved his mouth towards her in a final kiss goodnight.

TWELVE

It wasn't like Brooke to be nervous, but as she waited for Liam to pick her up, she could feel her stomach doing somersaults. Silently, she sent up a prayer for God to calm her nerves and for everything to go well.

Liam pulled up in his SUV, then hopped down from inside and made his way over to her.

He looked handsome in a pair of jeans and a blue button-up shirt. His dark hair was styled like the night before, spiked towards the center with a minimal amount of gel, enhancing his hazel eyes.

"You look great in jeans," he said as he took in her own pair matched with an emerald green sweater on top.

"Thanks," she said with a smile. "You look pretty good in your own pair."

"You ready to head over to my place?" he asked as he took her hand and lead her to the vehicle.

"Sure. What do you have planned?"

Liam opened the door for her. "You'll just have to wait and see."

As they drove down the road, they listened to a few Christmas songs on the radio. At first, they just listened, but by the second song, they were both singing along to the familiar words.

A couple minutes later, they arrived at a snow-covered cabin with a large barn next to it. Liam jumped out and came around to help her down.

"I figure, first things first, I would like to introduce you to my horses," he said, taking her hand and guiding her towards the barn. "If you're up for it, we could go horseback riding together."

"Haven't done it in a couple of years, but sounds like fun."

Once they were inside the barn, he led her over to the first stall. He reached out his hand, and the gray horse from her sleigh ride came into view.

"I recognize her from the first time we met," Brooke observed.

He chuckled. "There goes your cop skills again. You're right; this is Tinker. She's the first horse I bought. I use her a lot for sleigh rides because she likes people and is easy-going."

The horse neighed in response, almost as if agreeing with his statement about her.

"Can I touch Tinker?"

"I'm sure she'd love that. You might as well get to know her since I planned on putting you two together for our ride later."

Brooke reached out and placed her hand on the side of the horse's neck. She rubbed along the mare's coat as she said, "Hi, Tinker. My name's Brooke. Nice to meet you."

The horse neighed again, introducing herself in return.

"She likes a good scratch behind the ears," Liam suggested.

Brooke did what he said, and the horse leaned into her gesture.

From further in the barn, she heard some disgruntled moans.

"Come on, I need to introduce you to the rest of the guys. They sound jealous that Tinker is getting all the attention."

In the next stall was a paint horse. The patchwork of brown and white on the horse's coat was gorgeous.

"This is Bell. I got her from an auction. If she didn't sell, they planned to put her down because of her age. She seemed like she had a few more good years left in her, and I was right."

After spending a few minutes with Bell, they made their way across to the other stalls. There was a large, brown horse in the next stall.

"This is Peter. He was the second horse I got. I got him because he's strong and can do a lot of work before wearing out. He's ornery though, but we make it work."

When Brooke reached out towards him, the horse turned his mouth towards her and tried to take a bite. Before he could get a clean bite, Liam swatted at his nose and said, "No, Peter, that's not how you say 'hello'."

Brooke yanked her hand back and said, "I think I'll keep my distance from him for a while."

"Probably a good idea," Liam agreed.

In the final stall, there was another gray horse. This one also had a few black spots and a blaze in the center of his forehead.

"My final horse is Pan. He was the last horse I got. I probably use him the second-most for rides next to Tinker."

Brooke thought about the names and recited them in her head. *Tinker, Bell, Peter, Pan.* She realized the connection. "All the names are from *Peter Pan*. Are you a Disney fan?"

He reached out and patted Pan. After a moment, he answered. "My wife was a huge one. She introduced me to that world. My parents were more into intellectual trips rather than for fun, and they didn't believe in TV or movies. I never even knew what Disney was until I met Linda. We actually spent our honeymoon at Disney World."

"So, you named the horses after the characters?"

Liam nodded. "I wanted to remember her by giving them names from her favorite movie."

"That's sweet, Liam; you must have loved her a great deal."

"I did. Part of me still does. I don't think that ever goes away."

Brooke reached out and placed her hand on his arm. "And it shouldn't. It shows who you are by how much you still honor her."

He changed the subject by asking, "You ready to saddle up the horses and go for a ride?"

"Sounds great."

A half hour later, they were each mounted on a horse and heading out along the trails on the east side of Clear Mountain. They meandered along the edge, talking about Christmas and what they did growing up.

"Most of the foster parents I had didn't care much about doing anything for Christmas. I was lucky to get a gift on Christmas morning. I had one set of parents though, when I was eight, who made the extra effort with a tree and a bike wrapped with a big bow."

"Wow, that sounds amazing. What happened with them?" Liam inquired.

"I was their first foster kid, and I stayed with them until they got pregnant a year later. They decided they wanted to focus on their own family, and didn't want to foster anymore."

"I'm sorry. That stinks."

"Yes; sometimes I wonder if it would have been better to never experience that one great Christmas. If I hadn't, I wouldn't have known what I was missing out on."

"Well, the good news is, you can build your own Christmas traditions now. You can have wonderful Christmases again, starting this year with me."

Brooke looked over at him and smiled. "I'd like that."

"Me too," he affirmed. "I have done nothing for Christmas since my wife died. I didn't feel like there was anything to celebrate until now."

They made their way back to the barn after a couple of hours on the trail. They rubbed down and fed the horses before going inside the cabin.

Once in the kitchen, Liam said, "I bought ingredients for marinated chicken breasts with potatoes au gratin."

"I'm glad you can cook, because I'm horrible at it," Brooke admitted. "I can make a cup of noodles, or toast a bagel, but that's about it for my kitchen skills."

"No worries. Sit back and enjoy a glass of sparkling cider while I make dinner."

Brooke watched Liam move around the modern kitchen with its granite countertops and stainless appliances. He was confident, moving from the sink to the counter, and then placing the dish into the oven.

Once the meal was cooking, he moved over and opened a drawer, pulling out a deck of cards. He came over and sat down across from her. "You up for a game of Gin Rummy?"

"I thought you didn't play a lot of games?" Brooke asked with a confused look.

"Oh, I said I didn't play a lot of board games, but Linda loved cards. We played often together, and also had a group we played with on the weekends. Plus, I also played poker with the guys from work once a month."

"I'm up for it. I need to warn you though, I'm awesome at cards, too," she said, taking the deck of cards from him, opening it, and bridging the cards as she shuffled them.

"Okay, sounds like it'll be fun," Liam said with a grin.

They spent the next thirty minutes playing cards while the food continued to cook in the oven. When the timer dinged, Liam was winning, but only by a few points.

"I think I would have caught you on the next round," Brooke said as she gathered up the cards and put them back in the box.

"You probably would have," Liam agreed. "Next time."

He stood up and moved over to the oven, then pulled out the chicken dish. As he lifted the cover, a fragrant smell of the herbs and seasoning wafted through the air. Next, he pulled out the potatoes which had been cooking on the second rack. He placed a chicken breast on each plate along with a serving of the potatoes, and a helping of green salad he grabbed from the refrigerator.

Liam carried the plates over to the table, putting one in front of Brooke and the other across from her where he took his seat again.

"Why don't we pray over dinner," Liam suggested as he reached out and took her hand. "Dear Lord, thank you for this wonderful evening. We remember that you sent Your Son to us, and we are so grateful. Bless this food to our body as well as our time together. In Jesus' Name, we pray, Amen."

Brooke picked up her fork, cut off a piece of her chicken, then popped it into her mouth. Her eyes grew round with appreciation. After she finished the first bite, she said, "This is so good. I can't believe what a great cook you are."

"Glad you like it," he said before taking his own bite.

They ate the rest of the meal as they talked about their favorite TV shows and music. It turned out, they enjoyed the same crime shows as well as a Christian radio station.

Once they were finished with the meal, Liam stood to take the dishes. Brooke stood up and reached out, stopping him. "No way you're doing the dishes. If you cooked, I'm cleaning up."

"Okay, I'll let you, but only because I want to go grab some more wood for the fire."

"Deal," she said, taking the dishes from his hands.

A half hour later, Brooke joined Liam in the living room where he was adjusting the wood with the metal poker.

"The counters are clean and the dishwasher is running," Brooke informed him, as she took a seat on the rug in front of the fireplace.

Liam scooted back to join her, wrapping his arm around her shoulders. "I have to tell you, this has been the best day I've had in a long time."

Brooke nodded. "It has for me as well. Thank you for inviting me over."

He tucked a lock of her hair behind her ear, then slowly leaned in and kissed her, causing Brooke to relax into his embrace. After the kiss ended, they continued to watch the flickering flames for several minutes.

"I don't want to leave, but I have to admit, I'm getting tired," Brooke told Liam. "Do you mind taking me back to the resort?"

"Not at all," he said, standing up and pulling her up beside him. "Besides, the sooner we go to sleep, the sooner we can wake up and share Christmas Day together after I pick you up again."

Leaning up on her tippy-toes, she kissed him on the lips. "I'm looking forward to it."

"Me too," he said, before heading out the door with Brooke by his side.

THIRTEEN

As they entered Liam's cabin, he excitedly ushered Brooke into his living room.

"What do you think of the Christmas tree?" he asked, hoping she would approve of the evergreen he had cut down on his property earlier in the morning and placed next to his fireplace.

"It's gorgeous," she said, rushing up to the tree and touching the edge of the limbs. "When did you have time to do this?"

"I cut it down before picking you up at the resort. I didn't decorate it though since I want us to do that together," he said, gesturing to a bowl of popcorn and thread. "Sorry I don't have real ornaments. Like I said, I haven't celebrated Christmas in a long time."

"Don't apologize. I'd love to make our own garland to hang on the tree," she stated, kneeling down by the table and picking up a string and a kernel of popped corn.

"Great," he said, joining her on the rug. "This makes me feel like a kid again."

She smiled at him. "It makes me feel like a kid for the first time. My foster families never did anything like this."

"Well, I'm glad we get to do it together this year."

They spent the next hour stringing popcorn and placing it on the limbs of the tree. Once they finished, Brooke excused herself to use the restroom.

While she was gone, Liam pulled a small package from behind the couch and placed it under the tree. When she came back into the room, he gestured towards it. "Look, there's something under the tree."

Brooke's eyebrow arched in surprise. "How did that get there?"

He shrugged. "I wanted to surprise you."

With a smile, she picked up the package. "Mission accomplished." She brought the gift over to the couch where she took a seat on the edge. Gingerly, she opened it up to reveal a small jewelry box. Inside, was a silver bangle bracelet with her name engraved on it.

"It's beautiful," she said. "Where did you get it on such short notice?"

"I made it last night," he confessed. "I took

metal shop when I was in high school, and one of the things we learned how to do was make jewelry."

She slipped it on her wrist and flicked it back and forth. "It fits perfectly."

"I'm glad," he said with a grin. "It looks really nice on you."

"Hold on," Brooke said as she jumped up from the couch and ran over to her purse. She pulled out a little brown paper baggy and handed it to him. "I have something for you too."

Liam reached inside and pulled out the contents. Wrapped in some napkins was an Origami dove. The folds were intricate and made the paper creation appear 3D.

"Did you do this?" he inquired with amazement.

Brooke nodded. "I told you I enjoyed puzzles when I was little. Well, Origami is like making your own puzzle. I checked out every book on the subject from the local library to teach myself. I still do it often on the weekends."

He moved the bird back and forth in his hand, loving the way the wings fluttered as he did it.

"I know it's not much, and maybe a little silly, but I didn't really have time—"

Liam raised his hand and shook his head. "No, I love it. I have just the perfect place for it," he stated as he got up from his seat and put it in the center of his bookcase on the left side of the fireplace.

"You ready for brunch?" Liam asked as he made his way into the kitchen and opened the door of the oven where he had kept the casserole he made for them.

"Sure. What did you make this time?" Brooke asked as she came up and peered over his shoulder at the glass dish.

"I made an egg and ham casserole."

"You never cease to surprise me," she said with a laugh. "You better watch out, or you'll spoil me. I doubt you want me to get used to this."

"I like cooking for you."

"Well, I won't be the one to argue then," she said, taking the plate of food he offered.

Liam made himself a plate, but before she could sit down at the table, he stopped her.

"Rather than sit in here, why don't we take our food into the living room so we can watch a Christmas movie."

"I love that idea," she said with a big smile, following him into the other room. "I love Christmas movies. Are you more of a, *It's a Wonderful Life* guy, or *A Miracle on 34th Street* fan?"

"Don't make fun of me, but my favorite is *National Lampoon's Christmas Vacation*."

"Really? I never took you for the slap-stick humor type."

"Oh no, are we going to have our first disagreement?" Liam asked, half-joking, half-serious.

She laughed, jabbing him in the side with her elbow. "No way. Lucky for you, I'm partial to comedies too."

"Phew, that's a relief. I might have to end things right now if you weren't," he said, laughing along with her as he took the DVD and put it in the player.

He joined her on the couch where he slipped his arm around her shoulders. She snuggled down into the crook of his arm and watched as Chevy Chase took to the screen.

An hour and thirty-seven minutes later, Liam stood and stretched. "Man, I don't think I've laughed that hard in a long time."

"Me either," Brooke agreed, joining him in a stretch. "It felt good."

"You up for going out with me and checking on the horses?"

Brooke nodded. "Sure, I'd love to see how all of them are doing." Then a skeptical look crossed her face as she added, "Well, all of them besides Peter. I'll keep my distance from him in case he still wants to take a bite out of me."

"Understandable, but I think he'll grow on you over time."

They made their way out to the barn where they could hear the horses shuffling and neighing with anticipation when the door slid open.

Liam made the rounds, checking on the horses. When he came to Bell's stall, a chill shot up his back as his brows drew together in worry. She was lying on her side, not moving. He flung open the door and rushed inside, kneeling down beside her.

"What's wrong?" Brooke asked from behind him.

"I'm not sure," he said as he placed his hand on the side of her neck. "She's really sick, but I'm not sure why."

He grabbed his cell phone out of his back pocket and dialed the number for the local veterinarian. Liam hated to bother the doctor on Christmas, but as sick as Bell was, he wasn't sure if she would make it through the night if he waited.

Voicemail. I hope he's not out of town.

"Hello, Doctor Furston, this is Liam Davis. I'm sorry to have to call today, but I've got a really sick horse here. If you're available, I need you to come check her out as soon as possible. Thanks."

He ended the call and turned to Brooke. "Do you mind praying with me for her?"

Brooke came into the stall and joined Liam on the

other side of Bell. She placed her right hand on the horse's neck and then took Liam's hand with her other.

"Dear Lord, we come to you Father, and we ask you to please help Bell get better. We're not sure what's wrong with her, but You know Lord, and we ask that You intervene. Please heal her, Lord. We know You can do all things, so please Lord, do this for us. In Jesus' Name, we pray, Amen."

A peace flooded Liam's spirit as he opened his eyes and looked over at Brooke. "Thank you."

"Of course. I love Bell. I want her to be okay, and I know God can heal her."

They spent the next twenty minutes next to Bell waiting for the doctor to call. When he finally did, he informed Liam he would come over in thirty minutes.

After a thorough exam by the elderly, grey-haired veterinarian, he turned to them with a concerned look on his face. "I hate to tell you this, Liam, but I think Bell is suffering from colic."

"How bad is it?" Liam inquired.

"The good news is, I think it may only be gas colic and could be from something she ate. Has she had a change in diet?"

"I tried a new source for hay. Could that cause this to happen?"

The doctor nodded. "You need to stop using that hay immediately and report it to who sold it to you. I'll examine your other horses, but I'm guessing it's affecting Bell first because of her age. I'll give her an IV of analgesic and some mineral oil and mild laxative."

"What can we do?" Brooke asked with concern.

"You need to keep an eye on her and give her some time to let the medicine fix what's wrong. Keep her comfortable so the gas can move through the intestinal tract. Once she's doing better, you need to get her up and hand walk her. I'll come back out in two days and check on her. If anything changes or she gets worse, call me right away."

Liam and Brooke both nodded their heads.

"Thank you for coming, Doctor Furston. I know it's Christmas and all, but I was really worried."

"You did the right thing by calling me. I know how much you care for your horses. My family understands."

The doctor took off and left them alone in the barn.

"I'm glad to hear Bell's sickness isn't as serious as you first thought," Brooke said as she helped Liam bag up the last of the bad hay.

"What are you going to do about food for the horses?"

"My regular supplier gets back from vacation tomorrow."

"That's good." Brooke scrunched up her face and pressed her lips together before asking, "Do you think it's all right if I stay long enough to make sure Bell is okay?"

Liam turned to Brooke, reached out, and gathered her into his arms. He placed his chin on the top of her head as he said, "It's more than all right. I'd like it very much."

"Good, it's settled. I'll finish the week out at the resort."

Though he was grateful Brooke would be staying for the next couple of days, he didn't know what he would do when it was time for her to return home to Boulder. Pushing the troubling thought away, he leaned down as he tilted her head up, claiming her mouth with his own and drowning out all the swirling thoughts in his head.

FOURTEEN

Two days had passed since Bell became sick. The whole time, Brooke and Liam spent their time in the barn with her, coaxing her back to health.

After Doctor Furston's follow-up visit, Brooke could tell Liam was feeling better about the situation.

"I was thinking, since Bell is much better, do you think we could take a couple of hours and go to church tomorrow morning? It'll be my last day in Clear Mountain before I have to head back to Boulder."

Even as Brooke said the words, disappointment seized her heart. Why did leaving Clear Mountain—correction Liam—bother her so much? She'd only spent a week with him, yet, she didn't like the idea of never seeing him again. *At least I will still have tomorrow with him. We can have one last great day together before I have to go back to the real world.*

"If you haven't noticed, I'm kind of a hermit. I haven't ventured much into town, so I've never found a church to attend."

"You know that's not good, right? You need to be connected with other Christians. Reading your Bible and praying is good and all, but fellowship with other believers is important too."

"After my wife died, I had a hard time getting close to people."

Brooke reached out and touched the side of his face. "That makes sense, but it doesn't have to be that way forever. You can take this small step with me."

He put his hand on hers and grinned. "Since you put it that way, I think I can manage."

"Let's go inside where I can look up a church on the internet," Brooke suggested.

"Great, and I'll make dinner."

As they stepped into the lobby of Clear Mountain Assembly, the friendly vibe along with smiling faces welcomed Brooke and Liam.

There were groups of people talking, but several stopped as they approached. Members of the different groups waved and said "hello" as they passed by. A bubbly redheaded woman was standing by a kiosk as they approached.

"Hi, my name is Deanna Harper," she said, reaching out her hand to shake each of theirs. "Welcome to Clear Mountain Assembly. Are you both first-time visitors?"

They both nodded.

"I'm Brooke Patterson, and this is Liam Davis," Brooke said in return.

"It's so nice to meet both of you. Are you new to the area?"

Liam shrugged. "Sort of. I've only been here a couple of years."

"And I live in Boulder. I'm just visiting," Brooke explained.

"Well, if you like it, I hope you will think about coming back. We have a couple of people that make the trip in from Boulder to attend church here."

"I have a church I attend in Boulder, but you never know what the future holds," Brooke said with a smile.

Deanna handed them both a church bulletin, along with a welcome card before opening the door for them to enter the sanctuary.

Once inside, they looked around for a set of seats. They found a couple towards the back. Just as they were getting situated, Brooke heard a voice from the side say, "I didn't expect to see you guys here." Officer Aiden O'Connell came into view with a pretty blonde woman on his arm.

Brooke stood up and reached out her hand to shake Aiden's. "It's good to see you, Officer O'Connell."

"Please, call me Aiden." He glanced next to her and gave a knowing smile. "It seems you found a reason to stick around even after our search and rescue the other day."

"I ended up spending the whole week at the resort." She glanced next to her at Liam, who stood to join her. "Liam showed me around."

"He's good at that," the blonde woman said with a smile. "He gave us a wonderful sleigh-ride and tour for our honeymoon." She glanced at her husband as her eyes grew round. "That's been almost two years now."

Aiden chuckled. "Time flies when you're living a wonderful life." He gestured to the woman next to him. "This is Lindsay, my wife. Lindsay, this is Officer Brooke Patterson, and you already know Liam."

"Nice to meet you, Brooke. It's good to see you again, Liam."

"Do you mind if we sit with both of you?" Aiden asked.

"No, that would be nice," Brooke said, moving back towards the seat to make room for them.

Just as they all were in their places, the musicians took to the stage and started the first worship song. Brooke enjoyed the music and was certain the pastor would deliver a great message.

After introducing the series, the pastor got into the core point of the sermon. "God designed each of us the way we are. Often, we view our flaws as our greatest weaknesses, but the truth is, God designed us with them so He can use them to help others, to teach us things, and to draw us closer to Him. Our worst flaws can be our biggest strengths if we let God work in our lives."

Brooke liked what the pastor was saying. Her own childhood came to mind. She had always lived her life like it was this huge flaw, but now she wondered if she could use it to help other kids in similar situations. Maybe, she could volunteer at some group homes.

Once the service was over, the two couples stood and headed into the lobby.

"You both should come to lunch with the rest of us," Lindsay offered. "My friend Erica, is coming along with Deanna, who you probably already met when you got here."

Both of them nodded as Aiden added, "Yes, Deanna's super-social so being a greeter is the perfect volunteer spot for her."

Everyone laughed for a few moments until Deanna joined them. She glanced around the group, then asked, "What's so funny?"

Instantly, Aiden stopped laughing.

"Nothing," Aiden said defensively. "I don't want to make my dispatcher mad and end up with horrible calls all next week."

"You work for the police department here too?" Brooke asked with surprise.

Deanna nodded. "Why?"

"Oh, I'm just happy to find so many people involved with law enforcement go here," Brooke explained. "It's not like that at the church I go to in Boulder, or the substation I work at, for that matter."

"Well, Aiden will have one more local officer attending Clear Mountain Assembly here real soon," a young brown-haired man with blue eyes said as he approached the group. Next to him was a woman with long brown hair and matching eyes.

"Did you get the transfer?" Aiden asked with excitement.

The man nodded with enthusiasm. "I did. You're right, they wanted me for my SWAT training."

"That's great, Connor. I bet you're so happy, Hayley, to have him in town permanently," Lindsay said as she reached out and hugged the other woman.

"I am. Not saying we didn't learn a lot from our time dating long-distance, but I'm ready to be in the same area code full-time," Hayley said with a smile.

"I'm sorry. It's so rude of us," Lindsay said, looking over at Liam and Brooke. "Let me introduce everyone. This is Hayley Hall and Connor Bishop," she said gesturing to the newest couple to join them. "Hayley, Connor, this is Officer Brooke Patterson and Liam Davis."

Everyone said hello and shook hands.

"So, Lindsay said you're an officer. What department?" Connor asked with curiosity.

"I work out of the Southeast Boulder substation."

"Oh, that's cool, I work out of the Northwest Boulder substation. Well, at least until next week when I'm transferring here."

"That's great. Aiden mentioned a position was available. Sounds like you'll be happy in it," Brooke said, trying to hide her disappointment.

With how much she liked Liam and the church, she had been contemplating transferring to Clear

Mountain. She'd always been partial to small towns and had wanted to raise a family in one. Now, it seemed the choice to transfer had been taken off the table. Did that mean she wasn't supposed to pursue things with Liam?

"Oh, his position is different. They want him to head up making a local SWAT team since Clear Mountain has been growing so much. The general officer position I mentioned is still available. Why? Have you thought about it? Are you interested?" Aiden asked.

Was Brooke interested? She had been thinking about it the more time she spent with Liam, but was she willing to give up her life in Boulder to start a new one in Clear Mountain? And was it reckless of her to even be thinking about it after one week of knowing someone?

Brooke avoided the probing questions. "Someone mentioned lunch. Where are we headed?"

"There's a great Chinese place over at the Riverwalk," Deanna suggested.

"That sounds perfect," Lindsay said. "I'll go tell Erica. She's in the back talking with some junior high kids who got into trouble."

The group headed to the restaurant. On the drive over, Liam asked, "I noticed you avoided answering Aiden's question. Are you interested in taking the position at the police station in Clear Mountain?"

Brooke pressed her lips together while she debated how to answer. "Ever since Aiden brought it up, I thought about what it would be like to live in a small town. I always imagined myself raising a family in one because I hated living in Boston. When I got the job with the Boulder police station, I figured I would just have to make do living in a big city. Now, I'm not sure."

"You're the one who told me, you can change. All you have to do is take one step. This could be your step."

"Do you want me to take that step? It's pretty quick. We've only known each other a week."

"Sometimes, when you know, you know. I've always made quick decisions, from when I was a day trader making deals, to when I accepted the Lord into my life, to when I asked Linda to marry me, or even when I moved out here to Colorado. I just went for it. The question is, are you the same? There's nothing wrong if you're not, and I'm willing to do the long-distance thing if you are."

"I'm glad you've made it clear where you stand. It helps to know you are serious about us. I wasn't even sure if what was going on with us was just a vacation thing."

"No, I really like you, Brooke. I want to see where this can go, but I'm not pressuring you to decide right now. Just think about it," Liam requested.

When they arrived at the restaurant, the hostess seated the group in the back room. They ordered family style, providing plenty of options for everyone to enjoy.

Brooke had a wonderful time talking with the women over the meal. Though she would miss not seeing Trina and Kristen every week, she could equally see herself enjoying life with the people sitting around the table. She even found out Lindsay was a social worker and could help Brooke volunteer at the local Clear Mountain group home.

She could have everything she wanted if she was willing to take a chance. Could she do it? Brooke wished she had the answer, but something was holding her back. Silently, she sent up a prayer, asking God to guide her decision.

FIFTEEN

As Liam hitched up Pan to the sleigh, Brooke came up beside him and watched. "I'm glad Bell is doing so well."

"Me too. She had me terrified there for a while," he said as he patted Pan and placed the bit into his mouth.

"You're great with horses. It's like you're doing exactly what you were always meant to be," Brooke stated as Liam helped her up into the sleigh before jumping up into the driver's side.

"Kind of ironic, because back when I worked on Wall Street, I never even had a pet, let alone thought my life would revolve around animals in my future."

"Life has a funny way of working out sometimes. Take us for instance, I never would have thought I would meet someone while on vacation that made me rethink my plans for the future."

Liam's eyebrows shot up in surprise. "How so?"

"Well, I never thought I was one for a long-distance relationship, but here I am thinking if we made the effort, we could make the commute between Clear Mountain and Boulder work."

"You're right," Liam agreed. "I can come visit during the week while it's slow and you can come up here on the weekends. And when you're ready, you can always transfer to the Clear Mountain station."

"I can tell you want me to take a chance and make the leap, but I'm not that way. I'm not saying never; I'm just saying not right now."

"I understand you being cautious. It's probably why I'm attracted to you. You know—opposites attracting and all."

"I like hearing you're attracted to me," she said, as she leaned over and placed a kiss on his cheek.

He turned his face to the side and leaned over to catch her mouth with his own. "Oh no you don't. I'm not settling for just a peck."

A few minutes later, he pulled the sleigh to a stop near a clearing. He pulled out a picnic basket and handed it to Brooke, then he grabbed a couple of chairs and a small table, setting them in the clearing.

As a final touch, he brought out two blankets and handed one over to Brooke.

They both took their seats, then Liam opened the picnic basket and pulled out the contents. He placed the sandwiches, chips, and bottles of iced tea on the table.

"I went simple this time. Hope you don't mind the basics for lunch."

"Hey, as long as I don't have to cook it, I'm content with whatever you decide."

"Good to know," he said with a grin. "I'll file that information away for planning our future dates."

"I like the sound of that," Brooke stated with a smile.

"Of what?"

"When you said, 'our future dates.' I've been indecisive about how to handle all of this, but I really want this to work between us."

"I can see that," he said, reaching out and taking her hand in his own. "I do, too."

After they finished their meal, they packed up the contents and returned for the final sleigh ride back to Liam's cabin. Along the journey, Liam wanted to say something to break the uncomfortable silence that had built between them due to Brooke's upcoming departure. Neither of them wanted to talk about her leaving, even though she had to return to Boulder for work tomorrow.

Brooke led Pan back into his stall while Liam put away the sleigh. They checked on Bell before heading into the cabin.

"How are you getting home?" Liam asked with curiosity.

"Oh, I already arranged for Kristen to meet me at the resort. She'll be there in," Brooke pulled out her phone and glanced at it, "one hour, which means you need to take me back there."

Liam nodded. "I'll be right back."

He headed down the hall and entered his bedroom where he grabbed his keys from the top of his dresser along with a small box he placed in his pocket.

Back in the living room, he asked, "You ready to head out?"

Brooke glanced around the cabin, then nodded as she grabbed her purse and coat. "Yes, it's time."

They drove the short distance to the resort in silence. Once they got there, Liam hopped out of his SUV and came around to help Brooke down.

She moved towards the front entrance of the lodge when Liam reached out and stopped her.

"I want to give you something." He pulled the box out of his pocket and handed it to her.

"What is it?"

"Open it," Liam coaxed.

Brooke did as he requested. Inside, was a metal heart on a chain. "Did you make this too?"

He nodded. "It's to match the bracelet I gave you at Christmas."

"It's beautiful," she whispered.

"Flip it over."

On the back, her fingers caressed the words Liam had engraved on the necklace for her. She read the words out loud, "Always Yours." Her eyes flew up to meet his. "Do you mean it?"

"I do. I wanted you to know how committed I am to you—to us."

"I love it," she said, reaching out and wrapping her arms around his neck. "Can you help me put it on?" she asked as she handed him the box, then lifted her hair out of the way.

Liam placed the necklace around her neck and fastened the clasp. As her hair fell down and around her shoulders, Liam couldn't help but admire how great she looked.

"Thank you," she whispered. "I'll wear them both while we're apart."

"Good. I want you to keep thinking about me until we're together again." He leaned forward and kissed her lips, savoring the feel of them against his own, knowing the memory may have to last him far longer than he liked.

Brooke broke the kiss. She stepped back, turned, and disappeared through the doors into the Clear Mountain Resort lobby. As he watched her leave, Liam couldn't help but feel a piece of him go with her. He didn't care what it took, he would convince Brooke Patterson to move to Clear Mountain.

EPILOGUE

Three months later.

Grateful the last box was finally inside her new apartment in Clear Mountain, Brooke let herself fall onto the sofa, which was against the living room wall, shoved out of the way.

"We're finally all done," Liam said as he joined her. "I had no idea it would be this hard to move you here."

She turned her head and raised an eyebrow in disbelief. "Really? After three months of convincing me to take the job at the Clear Mountain substation, now you're complaining about the work to make it possible?"

"Wow, Brooke's been living here less than a day,

and already fighting?" Aiden asked with a smirk as he came and took a seat in a chair.

"I wouldn't say we're fighting. More like heatedly disagreeing," Liam defended. "Are you trying to say you never do that with Lindsay?"

"Oh, he does all right. Don't let him tell you any different," Lindsay interjected as she joined them in the room. "I got a text from Hayley and they're waiting for us over at Sushi Mon."

Brooke stood up and stretched, looking around her new apartment filled with all her packed possessions. "Okay. I can deal with the rest of this after dinner."

"We'll meet you guys there," Aiden said, as he took his wife's hand and led her out the door.

Liam turned to Brooke and gave her a grin. "Just so you know, I wasn't complaining. I would move all your contents a hundred times over if it meant I got to see you every day."

"You know just what to say to make me let go of my anger. That's not fair; I'll never be able to stay mad at you."

Pulling her into his arms, he leaned towards her and whispered, "Good. All I want to do is live happily-ever-after with you, anyway."

His lips came down to meet hers in a passionate kiss. It felt wonderful to hold her in his arms and know he didn't have to worry about her leaving to go back to Boulder ever again.

"I love you, Brooke. I'm so glad you decided to move to Clear Mountain."

"I love you, too. I'm ready to start our lives together."

Liam took Brooke's hand and led her from the apartment. As they headed to meet their friends, he realized they were both ushering in a new life filled with the promise of joy and love.

A NOTE FROM THE AUTHOR

I hope you have enjoyed *Lawfully Dashing* and plan to continue to read more from The Lawkeeper series. Your opinion and support matters, so I would greatly appreciate you taking the time to leave a review. Without dedicated readers, a storyteller is lost. Thank you for investing in my stories.

Jenna Brandt

ALSO BY JENNA BRANDT

The Lawkeepers Series

Lawfully Loved

Lawfully Adored

Lawfully Wanted

Lawfully Wedded

Lawfully Treasured

Lawfully Dashing

Lawfully Forgiven

The Rockwood Springs Series

Promised to a Soldier

Courted by a Soldier

Second Chance with You Series

Rekindled

Match Made in Heaven Series

Royally Matched

Standalone Book

Waiting on the Billionaire

The Window to the Heart Saga Trilogy

The English Proposal (Book 1)

The French Encounter (Book 2)

The American Conquest (Book 3)

Spin-offs

The Oregon Pursuit (Book 1)

The White Wedding (Book 2)

The Christmas Bride (Book 3)

The Viscount's Wife (Book 4)

The Window to the Heart Saga Trilogy Box Set

The Window to the Heart Saga Spin-off Books Box Set

For more information about Jenna Brandt visit her on any of her websites.

www.JennaBrandt.com

www.facebook.com/JennaBrandtAuthor

www.twitter.com/JennaDBrandt

Signup for Jenna Brandt's Newsletter

ACKNOWLEDGMENTS

My writing journey would not be possible without those who supported me. Since I can remember, writing is the only thing I love to do, and my deepest desire is to share my talent with others.

First and foremost, I am eternally grateful to Jesus, my lord and savior, who created me with this "writing bug" DNA.

In addition, many thanks go to:

My husband, Dustin, and three daughters, Katie, Julie, and Nikki, for loving me and supporting me during all my late-night writing marathons and coffee-infused mornings.

My mother, Connie, for being my first and most honest critic, now and always. As a little girl, sleeping under your desk during late-night deadlines for the local paper showed me what being a dedicated writer looked like.

My angels in heaven: my grandmother, who passed away in 2001; my infant son, Dylan, who was taken by SIDS four years ago; and my father, who left us a few years back.

To my ARC Angels and Beta Bells for taking the time to read my story and give valuable feedback.

To the Jenna Brandt Books Street Team, who have pounded the virtual streets on the internet, helping to spread the word about my books. Your dedication means a great deal.

ABOUT THE AUTHOR

Jenna Brandt graduated with her BA in English from Bethany College. She is an ongoing contributor for The Mighty website, and her blog has been featured on Yahoo Parenting, The Grief Toolbox, ABC News and Good Morning America websites.

Writing is her passion, with her focus in the Christian historical and contemporary romance genres. Her books span from the Victorian to Western eras as well as modern times with elements of romance, suspense and faith.

Jenna also enjoys cooking, reading, and spending time with her three young daughters and husband where they live in the Central Valley of California. Jenna is also active in her local church, including serving on the first impressions team and writing features for the church's creative team.

Printed in Great Britain
by Amazon